Hope

Hope

LOUANN GAEDDERT

A Jean Karl Book
Atheneum Books for Young Readers

Atheneum Books for Young Readers
An imprint of Simon & Schuster Children's Publishing Division
1230 Avenue of the Americas
New York, New York 10020

Book design by Angela Carlino

The text of this book is set in 12.5 Adobe Caslon

First edition

Printed in the United States of America

10 9 8 7 6 5 4
ISBN 0-689-80128-9

Library of Congress Cataloging-in-Publication Data
Gaeddert, LouAnn Bigge.
Hope / by LouAnn Gaeddert. — 1st ed.
p. cm.
"A Jean Karl book."
Summary: In 1851 orphans Hope and John are placed in a community of Shakers, where they encounter a way of life that is strange yet comfortable.
ISBN 0-689-80128-9
[1. Shakers—Fiction. 2. Orphans—Fiction.] I. Title.
PZ7.G118Ho 1995
95-2704 CIP
[Fic]—dc20 AC

ATHENEUM BOOKS BY LOUANN GAEDDERT

Breaking Free

Hope

A mere *thank you* is insufficient to express my gratitude to those who helped create an authentic background for this story:

The authors, illustrators, photographers, and publishers of so many books about the Shakers. Each was useful in its own way.

The director, staff, and volunteers at Hancock Shaker Village. Over the years these dedicated people have preserved and restored the village, and expanded its programs for visitors. They welcomed and encouraged me, and opened the treasures of their library for my use.

June Sprigg, author and scholar. She generously shared her insights with me and checked my manuscript for historical accuracy.

1

Hope Douglas glanced quickly at the large woman called Sister Lydia, and then away. She wasn't Hope's sister, or John's. She wasn't Uncle Josiah's sister either. Hope pressed her lips together and stared steadily at the row of chairs hanging from pegs on the wall behind the sister. Although the office room was large, there was only one chair on the floor where chairs belong; Sister Lydia Hoyt was sitting on it. There was also one table and one candle stand.

Hope had heard about these peculiar people called Shakers. They owned many acres of land and they had big barns and shops and houses—all neat and well kept, but too plain, like this room. They didn't believe in mother-father-and-children families. Instead they lived in large groups, all the Shaker men together and separate from all the Shaker women. Hope had heard that they did something wicked in their church; she didn't know what it was.

Although the Shakers didn't have children of their own, they took in other people's children. They made it easy for people like Uncle Josiah to get rid of children like Hope and John. The children were probably expected to work like slaves. Why else would the Shakers want them?

Hope had been unhappy living with Uncle Josiah's family; she knew she would be miserable here.

John Douglas swallowed painfully and reached out to touch his sister's hand. He blinked back tears and tried to still his trembling chin. Hope woudn't like it if he cried. Hope said that nine was too old to cry.

"Hope's a stubborn one, Sister," Uncle Josiah barked. "Thought she and the boy should go on living by themselves. I asked her how she planned to pay the rent. She thinks she's mighty smart, but she couldn't answer me that. You'll have your hands full with Hope, but she's big, as you can see, and strong ..."

Big and strong, like a horse or an ox he wants to sell? Does he expect me to show the lady my teeth? Hope didn't move a muscle except to open her hand so that John's hand could nestle in it, like a frightened bird.

"The boy has a sweet nature, but I'll tell you the truth. He's delicate." Uncle Josiah continued to bark. "We'd have kept them with us—they're my own brother's children—but the boy ain't never going to be up to the hard work of the farm. Better you should learn him an easy trade. Clock making, maybe. Clever with his hands, is John. The girl's thorny and sour, not like my own girls. My own girls is gentle little ladies, all four of them. All I can say for Hope is she took right good care of her ma, up to the very last. You need a nurse here in your village? Call on Hope."

"Both children are welcome here." Sister Lydia stood. She was as tall as Uncle Josiah and her shoulders were as wide. She looked straight into his eyes. "Thank you for bringing them to us. Leave their things in the hall." Her voice was low and lovely, like music.

"Don't have much. But the girl's got a gold locket. Expect she'll try to hide it from you. That's why I'm telling you." He turned, patting John's head. "You behave yourselves. Both of you." He glared at Hope. "I hear you've been giving these folk trouble and I'll be back here with a switch. I'll—"

"That will be all, Mister Douglas." Sister Lydia nodded toward the door. She stood quietly, her head bowed, until the door banged behind Uncle Josiah. Then she looked at Hope and smiled. "I'm one of the nurses," she said. "We are generally healthy but there have been times when we could use an extra pair of healing hands."

At that moment a little round man appeared in the doorway. His bald head was shiny and pink and edged with a fringe of white hair. His eyes, under bushy white brows, were sky blue. They twinkled as he entered the office. "I hear we have a pair of saints in the making, come to bless our village," he said.

"That's to be seen. Hope and John Douglas, meet Elder Grove Wright. The boy is said to be clever with his hands. The girl was a loving nurse to their mother, who died last month. They were brought in by their uncle."

"You wish you were somewhere else, don't you?" Elder Grove didn't wait for an answer. "Here in the City of Peace you will learn to rejoice as you do the work of our Father God and our Mother Wisdom. You may even find pleasure in the company of some of us old codgers and among young seekers like yourselves."

He paused for a moment and then he held

out his hand to John. "Come, I will show you the woodworking shop and then I will take you to the boys' house. For now, you will be busy going to school and making brushes. Later, when the school term ends, we may be able to use your clever hands in one of our shops. In the meantime, we'll see what we can do to fatten you up some."

John turned toward the door and then he turned back. "Where will you be, Hope?"

"I'll come with you, Johnny." She took a long step toward him.

The elder shook his head. "Nay, Hope. Here we keep men and women separate from one another. I expect you'd heard that?"

She hadn't realized that children were kept apart, too. "John's never been away from me, never in his whole life." She reached out and put her hands on her brother's narrow shoulders. He seemed to have become even smaller since their mother had died. "I'll see you at meals, and school, and here and there among the buildings...I'll come and tuck you in your new bed. I'll—"

"Nay." The elder did not raise his voice but he spoke the word firmly. "John will be living in the boys' house. You will be on the third floor of the brick dwelling. You may see each other, but only from a distance. You will not speak. Girls go to school in the summer;

the boys in the winter. Say good-bye to each other now."

Dismayed, Hope shook her head slowly. "What if he is sick? Sometimes he can't get his breath. I know how to rub his back to ease him. I know—"

"Should he become seriously ill, you will be informed," the elder said to Hope. "Of that you may be assured."

She hugged John close and lowered her cheek to the top of his head. Even though she closed her eyes tightly, a tear seeped through her lashes.

John stood quietly for a moment and then he wiggled out of her arms and put his hand in the elder's hand. He left her—without a tear or a protest. She was his sister, the only person he knew in this strange place, and yet he went off *willingly*.

"Sit down, child." Sister Lydia lifted a chair from the wall pegs, put it on the floor and guided Hope to it. "You have lost one family—"

"You're wrong. Pa will be back. Ma told me—over and over, she told me—to take care of John until Pa comes back. Pa and John and me. We are a family!" Hope was shouting; she didn't care. Shouting was better than crying. "When Pa comes back—"

"Your uncle said that your father left during the first thaw in 1850, which means he's been gone almost a year. Does he know about your mother's death?"

"I wrote to San Francisco, California. I told him Ma was sick. I told him to come home. He never got my letter. It's a long way from Massachusetts to California, all the way across the country. Or maybe he got my letter but then it was too late in the year to cross back over the mountains. They're very high and they have deep snow on them all winter long. Uncle Josiah wrote to him right after my mother died. He'll get that letter and he'll come home, first thing after the snow melts in the spring. He won't like it that you have taken my brother away from me."

Sister Lydia smiled. "You are a child, Hope, even though you have borne a grown-up's burden for some months. Now you can be a child again, in your new family. Here we are all children of our heavenly parents, who love us, as we love one another." The sister stepped to the door. "I'm going out to find a sister to help you settle into your new home. I'll be back in a few minutes."

When she was alone, Hope pulled a fine chain from the neckline of her dress and opened the gold locket that hung from it. Blinded by tears, she couldn't actually see the two tiny drawings, except in her mind. One was of her mother; the other of her father. She closed the locket and held it tightly in her hand. Sobs shook her body; a fire burned behind her eyes.

"Give me the locket, please."

Hope jumped at the sound of Sister Lydia's musical voice. She blinked back her tears and swallowed her sobs.

"Give me the locket," the sister repeated. "I will keep it here. When you're grown, if you decide to leave us, it will be returned to you. Now stand up and meet Sister Anna. She and Sister Lucy Jane Osborne are the girls' caretakers."

"I can take care of myself—and John. We don't have to wait until we're grown to leave. We'll be leaving as soon as our father comes for us."

Sister Anna nodded but she said nothing. She was almost as tall as Sister Lydia but she was shaped like a broom handle. Her dress fell straight from her narrow shoulders to her shoes. Her white cap hid most of her cheeks so that all Hope could see of her narrow face was a small straight mouth, a long thin nose, and two squinty little eyes. The bit of hair not hidden by her Shaker cap was dull brown. She stepped behind Hope, lifted the chain and locket from her neck, and handed them to Sister Lydia.

Sister Lydia was much older than Sister Anna. The hair that showed above her forehead was gray and white like the feathers of a speckled hen. She wrote Hope's name on a piece of paper, folded it around the locket and put it in one of the small drawers built into the wall. "If your father comes for you, and if he wants to take you away, and if you want to go with him, your locket will be returned. That is a promise."

Sister Anna lifted a blue cape from a peg near the door and placed it around Hope's shoulders. She pulled the hood up to cover her head. It was heavy and soft and warm. Hope snuggled into it as they walked out of the warm building into the gray cold. Set back from a broad center path were a dozen or more wooden buildings painted in several different colors. Most were two stories high with steep roofs, some were smaller. The path was edged with piles of snow and dotted with frozen puddles.

"Our home." Gesturing toward a huge brick building at the end of the path, Sister Anna spoke for the first time. Her voice was not loud but it was high and reedy, as if it came through her long nose.

"Which one is the boys' house?" Hope asked.

Sister Anna said nothing while they

picked their way around the puddles. Then she motioned to a two-story building painted golden brown. “There,” she said.

There was one building and some open space between where Hope would live and where John would live.

They walked all the way around the brick house and entered a door on the far side. “You will always use this door,” Sister Anna said.

“It’s just like the one on the other side.”

“Nevertheless, girls and women enter and leave through the door on the west side of the building; the men use the east side.”

“What if I were near the east door and it began to pour rain or sleet or hail?” Hope asked.

“You would walk around to the west door.”

“If I had a broken leg, would I still have to walk all the way around the building?”

“Yea,” Sister Anna said.

These Shaker folk couldn’t say yes and no like ordinary people. Instead they used rhyming words like *yea* and *nay*. Hope asked herself why. Perhaps because *yea* and *nay* are Bible words.

“Under no circumstance will you enter by the east door or use the stairs on the east side of the building.” Sister Anna turned and looked down her long nose at Hope. “There are reasons for what we do. Accept that.”

Inside, the house felt warm but it looked cold and bare. The wide hall was empty. The walls were white with wooden pegs like the ones Hope had seen in the office. The floors were smooth and shiny. The two walked up a flight of steps to another wide hall that was just as bare.

They were at the top of the second flight of stairs when a giggle and a guffaw suddenly pierced the silence. Sister Anna gasped, frowned, and strode quickly down the hall. At the last door she turned and took one long step forward and stood with her elbows cupped in her bony hands.

From behind Sister Anna, Hope could see a corner room with four windows and six narrow beds—and pegs on the walls. Three girls stood with their heads together. Another sat, stern and stiff, on a straight-backed chair in the opposite corner. Between them, a little girl lay on one of the beds, sucking her thumb.

"I call the other one Sister Cackle. She sounds like a chicken and her neck is so skinny and wrinkled she looks like one." The speaker was a tall girl with red curls like tightly coiled springs. "I wouldn't want to be the one to eat a tough old bird like her." She guffawed loudly.

"I wouldn't either." A short, plump girl copied the older girl's guffaw.

Saying nothing, the third girl stepped away from the other two. When she saw Sister Anna in the doorway, she gulped and covered her mouth with her hand, as if to hide the smile on her lips, or to wipe it away. The other two snapped their mouths shut and sprang apart. The redheaded girl lifted her chin defiantly. The other blinked her big eyes rapidly and trembled. The little girl on the bed continued to suck her thumb. The girl in the straight-backed chair smirked.

Sister Anna stepped to the center of the room and stood with her head bowed and her hands clasped in front of her.

Hope waited as one waits for the thunder that follows lightning.

At last Sister Anna raised her head. "I remind you of our Millennial Laws, Section Six, Order Seven. I quote: 'All telling of falsehood, evil speaking one of another, backbiting or tattling, are utterly forbidden by the gospel.' Repeat after me: 'Evil speaking one of another, backbiting or tattling, are utterly forbidden.' "

The three girls muttered the sentence.

"Lift your heads and speak clearly." When the girls had done as she commanded, Sister Anna turned to Hope. "And now I want you to welcome Hope Douglas."

* * *

"Did you bring anything with you?" Elder Grove Wright asked John as they left the office.

John shook his head. "Uncle Josiah said we wouldn't need anything here. He said his own boy could wear my clothes—and use my knife."

John had let Uncle Josiah take the knife Pa had given him. He wasn't brave like Hope. She had stamped her feet and screeched when Uncle Josiah asked for her locket. John looked up to see if the old man was cross because he didn't have anything but what he wore.

"No matter. We'll supply your needs. Now step in here and take a look at this workshop." The elder lifted a heavy iron latch and guided John into a large room with a high ceiling.

John sniffed the perfume of raw wood and crept toward a workbench where a man was smoothing the edge of a long board.

The elder introduced John to the man at the workbench and to one who was sanding a leg for a chair and to another who was studying plans for a drawer to hold spools of thread.

There were other workbenches in the room. One had been made for the use of left-handed carpenters. John was left-handed. There were more tools in that one room than John had seen in his whole life.

"What do you think, John?" the elder asked.

"I think..." John couldn't find the right words to describe the wonders in this room. "I think it's all..."

"Grand? Delightful?" The elder's eyes twinkled.

"Amazing, too." That was the right word. "Amazing."

"You're going to find many things to like here. Come, it's time for me to turn you over to a caretaker at the boys' house. It's been my great pleasure to make your acquaintance, John Douglas."

At the end of the day, John lay in a narrow warm bed and thought back to the morning. The ride in the back of Uncle Josiah's wagon had been long and bumpy and sad. John had been sad for a long time. He had been sad when Pa left and when Ma was sick and when Ma died. He had been sad at Uncle Josiah's and then he'd been sad to be leaving Uncle Josiah's. He wished that things would stay the same so he'd know what to expect from one day to the next.

In the late afternoon, they had come to this place, where one surprise had followed the next. Hope said that nine was too old to cry, but she had cried when they said good-bye to each other. That was a surprise.

The elder's name, Grove Wright, was a surprise. A grove is a field of trees, not a man's name. The elder looked like the grandpa John wished he had. His eyes twinkled and when he talked to John he looked into his face, not over his head. And Elder Grove Wright had taken him to the wondrous woodworking shop, another surprise.

The boys lived on the second floor of a large golden house. On the first floor was a shop where the boys made brushes and brooms. Before supper, he had met so many boys he couldn't keep them straight, except for one who was about his age. His name was Calvin Fairchild. His hair was so light it was almost white and his eyes were the color of blueberries.

There were two caretakers. Brother Harry was young and sturdy looking. His whole face was dotted with freckles and he grinned often. He had given John clothes. Although they were not new, they were clean and pressed and the jacket was soft and warm. The other caretaker was Brother Benjamin. His back was as straight as a board and his hair was slicked down so that his head looked painted. Brother Benjamin scowled and frowned. He was the teacher, news that made John think that he would not enjoy Shaker school.

Supper had been another surprise. They lined up outside of the dining room in a brick house that was bigger than any building John had ever seen. Then they walked in and knelt behind their chairs and prayed. When they rose from their knees to sit at the table, John discovered that they were not allowed to talk. There were lots of people in the room, nearly a hundred, Calvin said later. The men and boys were at one end and the women at the other. The women had come in through a separate door. He hadn't thought to look for Hope but she must have been there, too.

The food was good and there was so much of it. When John finished one glass of milk, Brother Harry poured him another. Later, Calvin told John that the supper they had eaten was not special. "Just wait until breakfast," Calvin had said. "Sausage, maybe, and potatoes and applesauce and pie."

John fell asleep thinking about breakfast pie.

At last the day ended and Hope, tired in both body and heart, crawled into the narrow bed that had been assigned to her. The room was chilly, but, to her astonishment, the bedding was warm. Someone had warmed it with a hot brick or an iron, as she had sometimes warmed Ma's bed.

The supper had been plentiful and tasty, but the foolishness that went with the meal was enough to ruin it. They marched to the table in silence, the men through one door and the women through another. Hope had stretched her neck until she felt like a goose. Finally she had caught a glimpse of the back of John's head. They all knelt before they ate.

Then they ate in silence. No one even said, "Pass the bread." And then they knelt again.

A strange thudding sound interrupted Hope's sleepy thoughts. She turned on her side, keeping the warm blankets up around her neck. Pale moonlight shone on the bed next to hers. A ghostly figure was kneeling beside the bed and pounding her fist into her chest. It was Eunice, making a big show of her prayers. She was not only thumping, she was also sighing and groaning. Already Hope didn't like Eunice. It was she who had smirked while the other girls were being scolded. Her hair was no-color brown. Her eyes were so light they were almost colorless. Her mouth turned down so that she looked sour, like a green apple, but her voice was sticky sweet, like molasses.

"You must always sit with your right hand on top of your left," Eunice had cooed, as if Hope had committed some terrible sin by sitting with her hands cupped over her knees.

Eunice had told Hope that she and her mother had "seen the light" three years before. They had walked barefoot all the way from her stepfather's farm in Lee to join "the heavenly throng." She had paused to give Hope a chance to congratulate her on her barefoot walk, but Hope had said nothing. Eunice could walk barefoot in the snow for all Hope cared, and she could thump the breath right out of her chest.

Disgusted, Hope flipped over to her other side and closed her eyes. She heard another sound in this room that had seemed so silent. The little girl, whose name was Emma Jenkins, was crying. Did she cry herself to sleep every night? Where was her mother? Hope made a small opening in the covers so that she could reach out across the cold space between her bed and Emma's. She groped in the darkness until she found the child's arm, which she began to stroke.

At last the child quieted and Hope could pull her hand back under the covers. Was John crying? Was there anyone to comfort him? Hope closed her eyes and remembered days when she and John and Ma and Pa had been happy together.

2

Hope hated Shaker rules, especially the one that kept her from John. Entering or leaving the dining room she had glimpsed the back of his head and a bit of his cheek. Not once in the two weeks they had been at Hancock had she looked into his face. Did he miss her? Did he, like Emma, cry himself to sleep at night? She didn't know, thanks to stupid Shaker rules.

She pitied little Emma Jenkins and she despised Eunice. Every night the prig knelt on the cold floor and thumped her chest and moaned and groaned. She said she was praying for a gift. Why? If she were to receive a present like Hope's gold locket, the sisters would take it away from her. So why pray for a gift?

Hope did her praying silently. Six times every day, when they all knelt in the dining room, she prayed that her father would ride into the Shaker prison and release his children—soon.

Among the other girls in the corner room, Hope liked Jemima, the one with the curly red hair, the best. She was the oldest. Until Hope had arrived she had also been the newest; she had come to the Shakers the previous fall.

Jemima expected to be the first to leave. "Come spring, I'll be shaking Shaker dust from my feet. Just you wait and see." She demonstrated by kicking her foot forward and shaking it violently. "I ain't about to be turned into a pious praying prig." She tossed her head so that carrot-colored curls popped loose from her single short braid. She twisted her shoulders until the Shaker scarf fell away from her bosom, already as large as a woman's.

"Who brought you here?" Hope asked.

"Me. I brought myself 'cause I had to get away from my pa. Beat me, he did. Fall's no time to look for a home, but on the first balmy day, I'll be out of here. Just you wait and see."

"Where will you go?"

"Boston, maybe. Or California. Someplace near the sea. I wish to see the sea, the sea I wish to see."

Hope laughed. "Me and thee, we wish to see the sea." More people like Jemima would make this place more bearable—until Pa comes, Hope thought. "If our pa wants us to live in California, maybe you could go there with us."

Jemima nodded, but she didn't say anything.

Rachel, age ten, was like a plump, bug-eyed puppy, eager to please but not very smart. One day, soon after Hope had arrived, Jemima had told Rachel to skip from one end of the hall to the other. Rachel skipped. Sister Anna caught her and reminded her that skipping was against the rules. Two days later, Jemima told Rachel that the rules had been changed and that everyone was supposed to skip everywhere they went. Again Rachel skipped, but Jemima got into trouble.

"Don't matter none," Jemima said with a grin. "The Shakers just scold. They don't hit, not even their dumb animals."

There was one other girl in the room. Her name was Catherine. She was Hope's age but she was no taller than John, and just as skinny. Still she looked healthy. Her cheeks were rosy and her black braids were thick and glossy. She had thanked Hope for comforting Emma, explaining that the little girl had been crying at night since January, when her older sister had died. "She misses Ellen."

Eunice had sighed dramatically. "Over and over I've quoted the blessed scripture to Emma. Mark, chapter three, verse thirty-five: 'For whosoever shall do the will of God, the same is my brother and my sister and mother.' " Eunice smiled her sticky smile. "I am Emma's sister, as I have told her, not once, but many times."

"She's only six years old," Hope said through clenched teeth. "Did you never cry at that age?"

Eunice shrugged her shoulders and walked away, her hands folded piously in front of her.

"Have you lived here long?" Hope asked Catherine.

"Yea. All my life. My mother was sick after I was born and she brought me here and the sisters took care of both of us. My mother died when I was two months old."

"Where's your father?"

"I don't know."

"Don't you want to find him?"

"Nay. Here I have many mothers and fathers and sisters and brothers. This is my home."

Hope pitied Catherine who didn't know what it was like to have your own mother and father and brother.

When she felt like being fair, Hope admitted that there were a few good things about Shaker life. The work was easy and the food was both tasty and plentiful. During the last months before her mother's death, Hope had stayed home from school. Every moment of every day had been filled with hard work. Her back and arms ached most of the time. Every night she went to bed tired. Every morning she woke still tired. Toward the end, when both food and money were scarce, she had also gone to bed hungry.

Here she helped the sisters, sometimes in the wash house or the kitchen. She had threaded dozens of needles for sisters whose eyes were growing dim, and she had hemmed towels and sewed on buttons.

There were other good things. Small black stoves kept the rooms warm. Her night-gowns, like her dresses, were plain but neat and comfortable. The dwelling house had not one single decoration, but it was always clean and there were lots of windows.

None of these Shaker comforts made Hope happy. She had not known how much she cared for the members of her own family until she was separated from them. Here she was one of fifteen girls who slept in three rooms on the third floor of the dwelling. Sister Anna and Sister Lucy Jane Osborne tended to the needs of the girls, but they didn't love them—not even the little ones—as a mother or sister would love them. Hope pitied the little girls; there were several who were younger than Emma.

Everyone talked about "Mother," but Hope soon discovered that "Mother" was Ann Lee, the founder of the Shaker society. She had been dead for more than sixty years. Mother Ann believed that Christ had come again, just as He had promised. He had come in the body of Ann Lee. Hope couldn't, and wouldn't, believe that. If Jesus had come again as a woman, Hope would have heard about it before this. The Shakers lived well but their ideas were dumb.

One Monday morning after breakfast, the caretakers gathered all the girls together. "This will be a week of preparation for Christmas on Saturday, March first," Sister Anna announced in her high, reedy voice.

"In March? Christmas in March?" Hope was so surprised that she spoke her thoughts aloud.

"In December we celebrate the birth of Jesus. Our beloved Mother Ann was born on February twenty-nine," explained Sister Lucy Jane. She would be the teacher when the girls' school started. The surprising thing about her was that she was younger than Hope's mother. Her skin was smooth and her features were just right. Even her eyebrows arched perfectly. She turned to look directly at Hope. "In years when February has only twenty-eight days, we celebrate on March first. It's a holy day so we will do no unnecessary work. Since Christmas will be on Saturday, we will have much to do preparing for it and for the Sunday Sabbath that follows. We will spend both days in worship and meditation."

Sister Lucy Jane continued, "In preparation for the holy day, you will each be expected to confess your sins to either Sister Anna or myself. We will be waiting for you in our room every day this week during the quiet hours before supper and after supper."

"What sins?" Hope muttered.

"None of us is flawless. Confession is a keystone of our faith." Suddenly Sister Lucy Jane smiled. "I'm sure you'll find something to confess, Hope. Put your mind to it."

"Your loud voice perhaps?" suggested Sister Anna. "Or your critical attitude? Your lack of gratitude for your place in our family?"

Hope wondered why she couldn't confess her faults silently, to God. Confession was yet another thing to despise about the Shakers.

The Thursday before "Christmas," Hope was sent to the kitchen to help. Her first job was peeling and cutting up potatoes and carrots. While she worked, she watched a sister with old hands who mixed dough, kneaded it, and set it aside to rise. Her face was hidden by her crisp white cap, just as her bosom was hidden by a crisp white scarf.

The caps were another thing that Hope disliked about the Shakers. They were like the blinders some people put on their horses. The wearer couldn't see to the side unless she turned her whole head, and she couldn't be seen by anyone who was not directly opposite her.

Hope liked the way the sister kneaded the dough. She was small and so were her wrinkled hands, but she pushed and released the dough steadily and vigorously, as if to the rhythm of a tune that only she could hear. When she had set one batch to rise, she started measuring flour for the next batch. Late in the morning, the old sister was kneading more slowly and stopping often to ease the stiffness in her shoulders.

Hope put her knife and pan of potatoes to one side and approached the old sister. "I could knead the dough for you," Hope said in a low Shaker voice.

The sister protested for a few moments and then stepped aside. Hope floured her hands and pushed her palms into the springy dough just as her mother had taught her. She hummed a tune to establish a rhythm. The song was "The Foggy, Foggy Dew." She sang the first few lines under her breath. But when she reached the line she liked best, "I wooed her in the winter time and in the summer too," her voice escaped from behind her teeth. All the sisters turned to stare at her. Embarrassed, she clamped her lips shut and sang the last line in her head.

The old sister, who was stirring flour into warm milk and yeast, turned so that Hope could see her smile. Her face was as wrinkled as an apple left too long in the barrel Hope returned the smile and then added more flour to her dough ball and continued to knead. When the mass was firm and smooth—"like a baby's bottom" is how Ma had described the dough when it had been kneaded enough—Hope slapped it a few times. The old sister took the dough from her, added a few more slaps, and put it in a deep bowl where it would expand as if by magic.

"You have been taught well," she said and smiled. "My name is Sister Josephine. And yours?"

"Hope Douglas. My mother made very good bread, or she did when we had good flour and yeast."

"Here we always have good flour and

yeast." Sister Josephine divided the dough she had prepared and gave half of it to Hope. They were kneading slowly when Sister Josephine began to sing a jolly song that began "By freedom invited and music delighted." She sang softly so that only Hope could hear.

They kneaded to the quick rhythm. As Hope became familiar with the song, she sang too, very softly. A woman working at the nearest stone sink joined them, and then one who was preparing meat for the oven. Everyone sang softly and in unison.

Hope and Sister Josephine kneaded bread dough all afternoon and again on Friday morning. Hope began to think that they were making bread for the entire city of Pittsfield. Late in the morning, Sister Josephine finally counted the loaves and said, "Enough."

After dinner at noon on Friday, Hope discovered that they had, indeed, been baking bread for the people of Pittsfield, those of them who were in need. One or more loaves went into each of the baskets lined up on the floor—along with vegetables from the root cellar, blocks of cheese and butter, eggs, slabs of ham, dried apples, dried corn, and beans.

"Do you often give away food?" Hope asked, thinking of the times she and John had gone to bed hungry. "What do the people have to do to get these baskets?"

"Yea. We give them at Christmas and at other times to anyone we know to be in need. Our problem is that we don't always know who needs our help."

"Why do you give your food away?"

Sister Josephine stared at Hope for a moment, as if she couldn't believe the question. "It's our duty—and our joy. We who are so blessed want to share with those less fortunate."

When some of the brethren had loaded the baskets into horse-drawn wagons, the sister in charge of the kitchen patted Hope's arm. "Good work," she said. "Mother Ann is well satisfied."

Hope climbed the stairs to the third floor slowly; she still had not confessed.

"Sister Lucy Jane told me to tell you that she would expect to see you before supper," Eunice simpered as soon as Hope entered their room. "Confession is like a tonic, so good for the soul."

"My soul doesn't need a tonic," Hope muttered.

"Oh, but it does. We have all sinned and gone astray. We must —"

Hope stomped out of the room to avoid the rest of Eunice's sermon.

She knocked on the door of the room occupied by the two caretakers. "I've come to confess that I don't like the idea of confessing to anyone but God. Not one bit."

Sister Lucy Jane leaned back in her rocking chair and smiled up into Hope's face. "Sit on this stool here beside me," she said. "Tell me about your earthly mother."

Surprised, Hope paused and thought for a moment before she spoke. "My mother was very beautiful—until she got sick. She was tall and straight and she liked to wear pretty colors. Her hair was heavy and the color of cornstalks in the fall."

"You are tall and straight and your braids are as thick as corncobs and the color of corn silks. You must look like your mother."

"Oh, I don't think so. I'm not pretty, but I'm strong."

"You will be a beautiful woman, Hope, which will be as God intended."

Hope shook her head sadly. She was too awkward and too cranky to ever be as lovely as Ma. "She didn't stay beautiful. She got so thin and her skin looked yellow and her hair was limp." Hope paused for a moment to hope that Sister Lucy Jane would stay beautiful forever. "I wrote to Pa. I told him to come home. But he never got my letter."

"What kind of a man was he?"

"He *is* a fine man. He laughs and tells stories. Everybody likes Pa. But he's had lots of bad luck. His sheep got sick and the rains came the day before the harvest. So he sold the farm and moved us to a little house in town and he went off to find gold. You just put a pan in a stream and the gold floats into it. That's what he said. My pa'll be here in the spring. You'll like him. Everybody does. Except Uncle Josiah. I don't think he likes any of us."

"We're grateful to your uncle for bringing you to us. One day, when you become modest and obedient and pure of soul, you will be a worthy Shaker."

"No, I won't. I don't like the rules and I don't like Eunice. She's a prig. And I want to see my brother, John. And I don't want to confess."

"But you already have."

"What do you mean? I haven't confessed anything."

"You have confessed that you miss your mother and that you long for your father's return and that you want to see your brother. You have said that you don't like our rules and that you dislike a member of the girls' order. I will pass on your confession to the eldresses. I will tell them that you have comforted Emma so that she can sleep. And I will tell them that

Sister Josephine says that you have a talent for making bread and that you have a lovely, true singing voice. Be tolerant, Hope. Know that our rules, though many, are neither unreasonable nor harsh."

On the following day, Hope was awakened to the sound of singing coming from downstairs. It was still dark night outside; the Shaker adults always got up while it was still dark, five thirty during the winter. Catherine said that, come spring, they would get up at four thirty.

Hope listened to the music for a few minutes. Then she wrapped a blanket around her shoulders and crept out of bed. When she felt Emma tug on her nightgown, Hope wrapped the child in a blanket and led her to the door and out into the hall. The hallway was dark, but gray light flickered up the stairway from below.

Hope and Emma crept forward and down the stairs until they could see the brothers on one side of the wide hall and the sisters on the other side of the hall. They were singing a joyful tune that Hope had never heard before. Wrapped snugly in their blankets, Hope and Emma sat on the steps and listened. The song ended. Another began. The men marched off toward one end of the hall. The women marched off toward the opposite end. Then they came back to the center stairways. The sisters marched down the stairs on their side of the building. Although she could not see them, Hope could hear the men marching down the stairs on the opposite side.

At the foot of the stairs on the first floor they sang a more somber song that had many verses. When it was over, they all marched toward the meeting room singing yet another tune. Their voices grew dimmer and then were silent. The silence lasted so long that Hope was beginning to think that she should take Emma back to bed. She was urging the little girl to her feet when the singing resumed. One song and then everyone seemed to be hurrying back to their rooms.

"Back to bed, Emma," Sister Anna said, and then smiled when they both jumped at the sound of her voice. "Get the fire going in your room, Hope, and then wash and put on your Sabbath dress."

After a breakfast of bread and fruit, the older girls marched with the sisters toward the meeting house across the road from their dwelling. Long lines of Shakers from the other Hancock families were marching along the road toward the meeting house, some from the east, some from the west. Catherine had told Hope that the Hancock Shakers lived in five separate groups or families, each with its own dwelling, shops, fields, and barns. There were the Second family, the East, West, and North families, and the Church family. Hope lived with the Church family, which had the most members and the most children.

Today, for the first time since Hope and John had arrived, all five families would worship together. There would be more than two hundred people in the meeting house.

At first they all sat on hard wooden benches, the women at one side of the room and the men opposite. The elder with the shiny pink head spoke to them in his quiet voice. Hope was too busy looking around her to hear what he said.

Hope had heard that Shaker church services were wicked, but on this day all the Shakers were sitting quietly listening to the elder. The meeting house didn't look like a church. There were no stained glass windows or velvet cushions, no altar or cross. The large room was as plain as the meeting room in the brick house where they had met the previous Sundays and every evening before bedtime.

When the elder finished speaking, a woman rose.

"Eldress Cassandana Brewster," Jemima whispered.

The eldress began to speak. Hope had never imagined that a woman would dare to open her mouth in church. She was so surprised that she listened as the eldress talked about Mother Ann as if the woman were her own mother, someone she knew very well, not someone she had never met.

When the speaking part of the service ended, everyone stood and moved the benches back against the walls. The women lined up in rows on one side of the room and the men on the other. Hope knew that they were going to sing and march. Hope marched forward and back and forward and back, as she had been taught. She joined in the singing.

And then Sister Anna took all of the girls to one side. Singers formed a group in the center of the room. The girls and everyone else began to march in a circle. The march became livelier, and then they were stepping and sliding and skipping. They were, in fact, dancing. Ma and Pa had sometimes danced—at home or in somebody's barn. They never danced at church! Uncle Josiah said that all dancing was sinful. Did he know that the Shakers danced? In church? Dancing was the wickedness she had heard about!

Hope was so shocked that she didn't notice when the little children arrived until she heard Emma squeal as she ran to join the end of the line. An old sister took her hand.

And there standing against the opposite wall was John! He was grinning in his dreamy sort of way. Had he gained weight? In just three weeks? Their eyes met. A lump rose in her throat; she had missed him so much! He grinned more broadly and then followed another boy to the end of the men's line circling around the singers.

Hope was scowling. John had almost forgotten how cross she looked when she scowled. Didn't she like it here where the food was so good and the rooms were so warm? Maybe she scowled because she couldn't be the boss. When Pa was gone and Ma was sick, Hope had been the boss.

Calvin motioned to him, and he joined in the line of men. At first John had been surprised at the way these people worshiped God. Then he had been pleased. The Sunday they had gone to church with Uncle Josiah, the minister had preached for two hours. Twice John had gone to sleep and twice his uncle had thumped his head with the side of his hand. Even the songs had been dreary.

Here children weren't expected to listen to long sermons. The songs were peppy and you couldn't go to sleep if you were on your feet marching. When you marched with your fingers open and your palms facing upward, you were gathering blessings. John liked to think about gathering blessings. When you turned your hands over, you were scattering blessings. He liked that, too.

Some of the sisters began to twirl, faster and faster. One fell to the ground, and the others twirled around her. A small woman whose face seemed to be sending out beams of light raised both hands into the air. She spoke in a small voice that seemed to come from a great distance, but her words were clear. "Blessed are they that do His commandments, that they may have right to the tree of life and may enter in through the gates into the city (Revelations 22:14)." Tears filled her eyes and she sank down onto her knees.

"Thank you, Mother, for this gift," several others sang out. "This gift, this gift of love and life!" Others joined in the singing. Everyone sang "Come Life, Shaker Life." It was one of John's favorite songs.

Gradually, movements slowed to a march—and then stopped. After a few minutes of quiet, they sang a farewell song, and Brother Harry led the boys out of the building and across the road to their rooms. They were expected to read or talk quietly to one another. That afternoon the members of the Church family all met in the meeting room in the brick dwelling for a singing meeting. Hope must have been there, but he did not see her.

The next morning it was too cold for the old people in the other families to travel to the meeting house for Sabbath morning services. The members of the Church family gathered in the meeting room of the brick dwelling after breakfast. They marched into the room and around a small table. On the table was a picture of the tree of life that the sister had seen during the meeting on Mother Ann's birthday. It had bright green leaves and bright red apples.

John stood staring at the sister's marvelous gift until Calvin guided him to his bench in the men's section.

Two weeks later the boys' school term ended. The first day John had been afraid of the Shaker teacher, Brother Benjamin. He seldom smiled as he stood stiff as a board, his hair slicked down against his head. During John's second day at the Shaker school, Brother Benjamin had ordered him to stand and recite the nine times table. Although his voice shook, John had said it perfectly, he thought.

"Close your eyes and stick out your tongue," the teacher had commanded.

I must have made a mistake, John had thought. Eight times nine? The answer is seventy-two. Or was it sixty-three? Timidly he had closed his eyes and stuck the tip of his tongue between his lips. Something was placed on John's tongue. Fearfully, John had drawn it into his mouth. A sharp sweet peppermint!

In his old school, the teacher had used a ruler

to rap the knuckles of anyone who made a mistake. Those who misbehaved had to stand in the corner. Sometimes they were whipped. Brother Benjamin scolded and often made a boy do his work over until he got it right. He rewarded good work with peppermints.

At the end of each school day, the boys who did not help in the barn or with the wood for the stoves had worked in the shop on the first floor of the boys' house, making brushes. Altogether that winter they made 360 brushes. Some would be used by the family, but most would be sold to outsiders.

Three days after the end of the school term, it was so windy John felt as if he were being blown from the boys' shop to the dining room in the brick dwelling house. Then it began to rain, and to hail, and finally to snow. The boys spent the days making brushes, inside where it was warm and cozy.

3

On Thursday, March 26, Emma disappeared. After breakfast, the little girls went to one of the rooms to learn new songs. Hope was sent to work in the dairy and spent the morning churning butter. She didn't think about Emma at noon, or even at supper. When it came time to retire and Emma was not in her bed, Hope was suddenly alarmed.

"Has anyone seen Emma? Was she at supper? Is she sick?" she asked the four other girls, who were getting ready for bed.

Jemima, Rachel, and Catherine shook their heads. "All we like sheep have gone astray," Eunice said with a sigh.

"What's that got to do with anything? Emma is not a sheep and I want to know where she is!" A lump of panic was rising in Hope's throat. "Maybe she tried to run away and is lost out there in the cold. The calendar says it's spring, but it is as cold as winter. Maybe she's sick."

Hope strode out into the hall and knocked on the caretakers' door.

The door opened a crack. When Sister Anna saw Hope, she opened the door wide and stepped back, inviting Hope to enter the room. "What is the matter? You look—"

"Emma's gone," Hope interrupted. "She's not in her bed. I haven't seen her since breakfast. She could be—"

Sister Anna held up her hand to silence Hope. "Emma has left us."

"What do you mean? She couldn't die. She was—"

"Her father came for her. We hated to let her go, but there is nothing we could do to keep her."

"Why would you want to keep her? She should be with her family. Keeping children away from the people who love them is cruel. You are—"

"Hush, Hope." Sister Lucy Jane, who had been kneeling beside her bed, rose and strode across the room. It was the first time Hope had seen her without her cap and she could not help smiling. Sister Lucy Jane's hair was a deep chestnut brown and it fell in waves around her shoulders.

Her eyes and her voice were stern. "You don't know what you are talking about, Hope. It is Emma's father who is cruel. We were doing all that we could to protect her from him. If you had seen him, ranting and raving. He even suggested that we caused Ellen's death. Believe me, we nursed that poor child tenderly and to the best of our ability." Sister Lucy Jane turned away, but not before Hope saw tears in her eyes.

"I'm sorry," Hope said, meaning that she was sorry she had accused the sisters of cruelty. She knew what it was to nurse somebody as well as you were able and then have them die. She was also sorry that Emma was gone.

When she was in her warm, snug bed, Hope tried to tell herself that she was glad she would no longer have to comfort Emma at night. Now she could keep both arms under the blankets. Long after Eunice had quit thumping her chest, Hope was lying awake trying not to think of Emma.

Hope was never alone. She couldn't go for a walk by herself. The privy had four holes for women and two for little girls so that even there she had no privacy.

She was never alone, but she was often

lonely. She had known Emma, an ordinary little girl who sucked her thumb, for just a few weeks. Nevertheless, Hope missed her. Now there were five girls in the room. Hope liked jolly Jemima. She despised pious Eunice. Rachel was too young and silly to be interesting; Catherine was too quiet.

Two girls who appeared to be close to Hope's age sat across the table from her at meals. Since it was against the rules to speak in the dining room, Hope knew nothing about them except that their names were Elizabeth and Justina Irving. They slept in another room on the third floor. Hope thought that they might become her friends once school started, but that was not to be.

On April 8, the silence during the noon-time dinner was pierced by the bang of one of the heavy outside doors. Booted feet clomped down the hall.

As two men entered the dining hall, one of them began to shout. "The sheriff's come with me to get me girls. Come now, Lizzie, Tina. No trouble. Me and your ma wants you at home."

Each of the Irving sisters buried her face in the other's shoulder as they clung together, sobbing. Hope could scarcely believe the behavior she saw with her own eyes. If her father had come for her, Hope would have jumped up from the table and run into his arms. He'd have held her close, and she'd have been so very, very happy.

Sister Lucy Jane rose from the table, but Mr. Irving pushed her aside. He grabbed Elizabeth under the arms, knocking her chair backward. He set her on her feet and shoved her toward the sheriff. Then he turned to Justina, prying her fingers from the shoulder of the girl sitting on the other side of her. He pulled her away from the table and smacked her across the face.

"Move!" Mr. Irving shouted to four brothers who stood in front of the door. "These here is my gals, and the sheriff and me is taking 'em home." He thrust folded papers toward Elder Thomas Damon, who had entered silently from the ministry dining room.

The elder said nothing, but the brothers went back to their tables and the elder opened the door and followed the sheriff, the girls and their father out into the hall.

The people in the dining room continued their meal. Later, as they were kneeling in silent prayer, they heard more shrieks, which gradually faded into the distance.

That afternoon, Hope and Catherine were assigned to candle duty. They went from room to room, replacing candle stubs with new long tapers.

"When my pa comes for me, I'll run out of here so fast you'll think I'm a bolt of lightning," Hope whispered when the girls were alone in the meeting room.

"Maybe your pa is different, not like Elizabeth and Justina's father. He lived here once, you know, he and his whole family. He left first, then their mother. One by one, the children left, until only Elizabeth and Justina remained."

"How many children were there?"

Catherine shrugged her shoulders. "Four girls, I think. And some boys. I don't know how many."

"Why did they come if they didn't plan on staying?"

"Maybe to have enough to eat. Elizabeth and Justina wanted to stay forever and ever. They told me so themselves. Did you see Mr. Irving hit Justina? Did you see that?" Catherine's pink cheeks turned red. "Did your father ever hit you?"

Torn between loyalty to her father and the truth, Hope lied. Catherine would never understand that all fathers—or all the fathers that Hope knew—smacked their children. "Spare the rod, spoil the child" is what the Bible said. "You've got to whip Hope"—that's what Ma said when Hope was sassy or disobedient. Pa never spanked her very hard.

When will you be here, Pa? Why haven't you written to us? Maybe he had written to them at Uncle Josiah's. Surely Uncle Josiah would send the letter on to Hancock. Wouldn't he? And the Shakers? Would they give the letter to Hope?

"Tell me the truth, Catherine," Hope whispered. "If the Shakers got a letter that was meant for me and my brother, would they give it to us?"

Catherine cocked her head to one side, thinking. "I expect so," she said at last. "Yea. They'd give it to you."

Later Hope asked Jemima the same question. "Depends on who here saw it first. These crazy people don't believe in families. Some of them might think your pa had no business writing to you."

Finally, Hope asked Sister Anna.

"Why do you keep asking foolish questions, Hope?" Sister Anna glared and turned away.

"Please answer me," Hope begged. "If a letter was sent to me, would I receive it?"

"Of course. You might not be allowed to keep the letter, but you would be allowed to read it. Why can't you believe that everyone here wants what is best for you?"

"Because your idea of best is not the same as mine," Hope muttered to herself.

* * *

One day several weeks later, Hope and Jemima and four sisters carried buckets and brushes and brooms and rags across the road to the schoolhouse. Hope's task was to clean out the desks. Which one had been John's? She found no clue, just chalk dust and paper crumbs. Wherever he had sat, she knew that he had enjoyed this room, with its maps and globe. Had John traced the route to California?

Hope was polishing a desk next to the windows when Jemima tapped her shoulder and beckoned her to the window. She pointed to a young man leading a team of oxen across the road toward them. "Handsome, ain't he? Name's Zeke." Jemima tapped her fingers against the glass. The young man looked up and grinned.

"Surely you've finished that window," Sister Anna said, as she strode toward them.

"Just checking with Hope here. Asked her if she could see any streaks. Do you see any streaks, Hope?"

Hope shook her head.

"Now I gotta make a trip outside."

"Outside?" Sister Anna repeated in her piping voice.

"To the privy. I really gotta go, Sister Anna."

Sister Anna pursed her lips together, then she sighed and told Hope to go, too. Hope followed Jemima to the door, disgusted with the Shaker rule that wouldn't let Jemima take a few steps to the privy alone.

"You go to the privy," Jemima whispered as soon as the door closed behind them. She ran across the yard to the fence—and Zeke and the oxen.

Hope took a few steps toward her. "Don't," she whispered. "We'll both get in trouble."

Jemima turned and motioned for Hope to go into the privy. Hope shrugged and obeyed. Why not? When she came out of the privy, Jemima was waiting for her near the door to the schoolhouse. She looked as satisfied as a cat licking her whiskers.

"Thanks, Hope. Won't be long now and I'll be shaking Shaker dust from my feet. Maybe I'll let you come with me."

"John, too?"

"Maybe. We'd be a quartet of runaways." Jemima grinned and ran back into the schoolhouse.

Bewildered, Hope stumbled after her. A quartet is four. What four? Zeke? Surely Jemima wouldn't leave with Zeke. It was one thing for the Shakers to keep men and women apart so that they couldn't talk to one another; it was another for a girl to go off alone with a young man who was not her brother, or even her cousin. Maybe she needed Hope to go along so she wouldn't be alone with Zeke. Doesn't make sense, she thought.

The next morning it snowed. In the afternoon it rained and then it snowed again all night. By the end of the following day the snow lay piled high beside all of the walkways. Hope was glad; Jemima was too fond of comfort to even think about leaving in nasty weather. Hope had time to think about going with her.

It was still unnaturally cool when the school term began. In addition to the girls from the Church family there were five girls from other families. There were also three girls who had no connection with the Shakers except that they lived on neighboring farms.

Two of the neighbors were skinny little girls in faded and patched dresses. Sister Lucy Jane told the older of the two how glad she was to see her again. She introduced herself to the younger one and welcomed her to the school.

Then she turned to the other neighbor, a tall girl in a lovely cherry-red wool dress. "And you, Fay? You have become a young woman since last we met." Sister Lucy Jane stood for a moment examining Fay from head to toe. The girl had a bosom like Jemima's but it was not concealed with a scarf. "Frankly, I'm surprised that you chose to return to school this year."

"I'm anxious to learn all I can, Sister Lucy Jane."

"Are you?" The teacher sounded doubtful.

"She could sit here by me," Jemima said sweetly.

Sister Lucy Jane shook her head. "Nay. I don't think that's a good idea." She directed Fay to a desk at the back of the room behind the little girls.

There were no boys in the schoolroom. Otherwise, Shaker school was like the other school Hope had attended. She had always been a good student. Sister Lucy Jane nodded and smiled when Hope read aloud on the first morning.

They ate lunch in the schoolroom. During the morning someone brought meat pies and crusty bread for all the Church family girls. The girls from the other Shaker families had brought their lunches in tin buckets. Fay's lunch was in a box painted with yellow flowers. The little neighbors took pieces of hard bread from their pockets.

"Oh my goodness," Sister Lucy Jane said when she had distributed the meat pies. "The kitchen sisters have sent us too many pies. We can't return them; they'd think we didn't like them. Perhaps you girls could help us." She put meat pies in front of the two little girls who had brought nothing but hard bread.

Hope smiled to herself. The Shaker sisters had many stupid ideas and lunatic customs, but they were kind to young children. She hoped the brothers were kind to John.

When they had eaten, the girls went outside and skipped back and forth across the yard. They didn't have toys, not a ball or a doll. Hope had given her doll to Uncle Josiah's youngest girl; she wished now she'd brought it for one of these girls. She wondered if Catherine had ever seen a doll.

Had Jemima noticed that they had no toys? She looked for her but she was nowhere in sight. Neither was Fay.

When Sister Lucy Jane came to the door to swing the hand bell, the girls lined up in order of their size, the smallest first. Jemima and Fay were at the end of the line. Sister Lucy Jane led the group in a fast march around the schoolhouse, down the road past the meeting house and back to the schoolhouse.

The next day, Sister Lucy Jane not only gave the little neighbor girls some of the good lunch from the kitchen in the brick dwelling; she also gave them a wooden box filled with food to take home.

Once again Jemima and Fay disappeared during the lunch hour. On the third day, Hope decided to find out where they went. She watched when Jemima rose from her seat, stretched, and headed toward the door. And then Hope rose too, but when she got to the door there was no sign of Jemima. She had to be in the privy, but she wasn't. Or in the woodshed. There was nothing in the woodshed except wood. In the boys' privy? That was impossible.

Hope stood beside the woodshed and waited. Sister Lucy Jane came to the schoolhouse door but Hope did not move until Jemima and Fay appeared from somewhere in the corner near the boys' privy. Jemima had a piece of straw stuck to her dress. Hope reached out and brushed the straw to the ground before Sister Lucy Jane could see it.

The next day Hope waited by the fence that separated the school yard from the new horse barn. As soon as Sister Lucy Jane began to ring the bell, Jemima and Fay ran from the barn and vaulted over the fence.

When Jemima saw Hope she hurried to walk with her. "Don't tell," she whispered. "Not if you want to go with us."

Elder Grove had said that when school ended they would find work for John's clever hands; he had expected to be sent to the woodworking shop. Instead he was sent to the barn to help out there while the older boys were all busy getting the fields ready to plant. Working in a barn meant cleaning up after cows. He didn't need clever hands to scoop smelly manure. Besides, he sneezed and coughed when he worked there.

Three other boys were also assigned to the barn. One of them was Calvin Fairchild. Of all the boys, John liked Calvin the best. He was just about John's age. No one knew for sure. The Shakers had guessed that he was two years old when they found him sitting under a tree near the brick dwelling. They didn't know who he was or how he got there. They took him in and named him Calvin after a favorite elder and Fairchild because they said he was a fair—meaning blond and pretty—child.

"Aren't you cross with whoever left you here?" John had once asked. "Most likely your ma was dead. My ma's dead. Maybe your pa was dead, too, or far away. My pa's in California. But somebody could have put a note on you. Said who you were. I guess you couldn't talk yet."

"I like the name they gave me and I like living here."

"You don't mind not having people of your own?" John had asked.

"The Church family is my family. The old ones are like my grandparents and the young ones

are my brothers and sisters. You're my brother, John."

John liked to think of himself as Calvin's brother, and he liked working beside Calvin. Even though he didn't much like the work, he liked the barn itself. It was another amazing place. Round with thick stone walls. Calvin said it was the first round barn in the United States. It could hold seventy cows plus some calves. Horses pulled hay wagons right into the top level so that hay could be thrown down to the cows on the level below. The barn was not dark and dreary like most barns; it had many windows and the wood beams made lovely patterns and shadows.

John admired the barn but not the cows. "They are so slow and so dull looking, and they make such messes." John sneezed.

"But they have beautiful eyes." Calvin laughed. "And they work miracles. They turn grass into milk. Could you do that?"

That was one of the things John liked about Calvin. He was almost always cheerful and sometimes he was funny.

Spring was advancing toward summer. When the girls' school started, the buds on the trees were just beginning to swell. The next week the tops of most of the trees were misty green as the leaves began to burst from the buds. The following week some trees were wearing their full summer garb. In the orchards, pink and white blossoms winked from the tops of the twisted apple trees. Platters of asparagus appeared on the tables in the dining room.

Jemima was still *talking* about shaking the Shaker dust from her feet, but she hadn't left.

Hope was becoming more and more anxious about her father. Every night she prayed that tomorrow he would come riding into the village to claim his children. Every morning she awoke thinking, this could be the day I will see Pa.

And then she began asking herself other questions: Is Pa riding around the Berkshire Hills looking for us? Has he already been here? Mr. Irving had come with the sheriff to claim his children. The Shakers said they wanted to keep Elizabeth and Justina because the girls wanted to stay. Were they also trying to keep Hope and John, who did not want to stay? Could they have lied to Pa? "What children? We don't know a boy and girl named Douglas." No. The Shakers were strange, but they were not wicked.

Maybe Uncle Josiah had lied. Maybe he'd made some deal with the Shakers. "You take these wretched children off my hands and I'll let you keep them forever." Maybe he'd never mailed the letter to California. What if Pa didn't know that Ma had died? That couldn't be! So where was Pa? Where was the letter he must have written?

4

The day they buried Sister Bessie Thomas was the day Jemima and Zeke chose to leave the Shakers. Hope and John were going, too.

Marching beside Jemima near the end of the long funeral procession, Hope tried to ignore her doubts. It was too late now to change her mind. All night her body had twitched as her brain darted from "what if" to "we must" like a thirsty mosquito. She didn't want to stay with the silly, silent Shakers. She hated their stupid rules. She had to find Pa—for John's sake as well as her own. If Pa had come back or written a letter, Uncle Josiah would know. They'd go to his farm first and ask about Pa.

What if Uncle Josiah hadn't heard from

Pa? Then they'd go back to where they had lived with Ma. The parson of the church there might have heard from Pa; he would put them up for a while and help them decide what to do next. In the end, they might have to go on to California to look for Pa themselves.

Deep down, Hope knew that it was foolish to think of setting out for California alone with John. Perhaps it was also foolish to trust Uncle Josiah to tell the truth about a letter from Pa. He might even take them back to the Shakers.

The plan was not wise, but she had to do something. She'd promised Ma that she would care for John until Pa came back, but John had been taken away from her and Pa had not returned.

At the head of the procession, four brothers carried a pine casket. Behind and around them was space that looked empty to Hope but that the Shakers said the space was filled with the spirits of Shakers who had died in the past. The spirits had come to take Sister Bessie to her home in heaven. Yesterday, Sister Lucy Jane had smiled happily when she announced that the old sister's heart had finally stopped beating.

"Aren't you sad that she has died?" Hope had asked, remembering her mother's death.

"Nay, Hope. Her body, which was giving

her pain, is dead and will be buried. But her spirit has escaped her old body and is free now to join the joyful spirits of Mother Ann and all the others who have gone before her. Some of the sisters will miss her, but we know that one day Sister Bessie's spirit will come to welcome our spirits. Why should we be sad?"

Hope wondered if Ma's spirit had escaped her body. All winter, Hope had been distressed when she thought of Ma's body in the frozen ground. From now on she would think of Ma as a spirit flying with the spirits of people she had loved, Grandma and Grandpa, and her aunts and uncles. She'd share that vision with John. She would tell him about the singing and marching and Eldress Dana's happy words remembering Sister Bessie.

Children under twelve were not allowed to attend funerals unless there was a special reason, so John was not with the brothers heading for the graveyard. Neither was Zeke, who had hidden when the brothers gathered for the funeral. Zeke would bring John to meet Jemima and Hope.

The sisters marched beside the road from the meeting house and then turned left on the path that climbed up to the cemetery. When they had made the turn, Jemima stepped out of the procession and knelt to tie her shoe. Hope stepped to the side to wait for her. That was one reason Jemima wanted Hope to come with her. If Hope didn't stop with Jemima, another girl or sister would. Hope was the only person Jemima could trust.

As the sisters marched on, Hope swallowed the fear rising in her chest. Jemima had said that this would be the most difficult moment, and Hope had promised that she could stand still and smile serenely. Except for scrunching her toes in her shoes, Hope was keeping her promise. She hoped that Zeke was keeping his. If he didn't bring John to the meeting place, then Hope would go back to the Shakers, which might set them to looking for Jemima and Zeke.

When the end of the line had passed, Jemima stood. The two girls walked to a huge pine tree and crept between its thick branches. They waited, scarcely daring to breathe, while the sisters marched on. When the last sister was out of sight, the girls lifted their skirts high above their ankles and ran across a stretch of open land to the row of tall trees and thick shrubs that separated the road from a cornfield. Bending low, they hurried on.

Suddenly Hope heard a rustle of leaves and then a thud. Zeke appeared at the foot of a huge maple tree just ahead of them. He grinned and then reached up into the leaves and lowered John to the ground.

"Where is it?" Zeke asked in a loud whisper.

Jemima walked around the tree and then she walked to a stone wall, smiling back over her shoulder. She said nothing but her eyes twinkled merrily. Then she knelt and reached under a bush in front of the wall.

"Hurry up," Zeke hissed. "We gotta get out of here."

"Don't rush me, Mr. Zeke." Jemima straightened up and thrust a tool into his hand. "You'll need this to dig up my fortune."

"Where?"

"Don't be so impatient." Jemima patted his arm and then she reached up and kissed his ear.

"Please, Jemima," he pleaded.

"You said it was me you loved, not my fortune." She pouted and walked away from him slowly. Suddenly she lifted her arm and pointed to a large white rock lying on the ground between the wall and the maple. "There!" She laughed aloud.

Zeke kicked the rock aside, dropped to his knees and thrust the tool, a small, pointed shovel, into the ground. He scooped up rich black dirt from which something glittered.

"Looks like gold," Hope whispered.

"It is gold. A gold piece. I buried it here, nice and convenient, before I went across the road and found me a home for the winter."

Hope thought about her locket. She

wished she'd had a chance to bury it. "Where'd you get the gold piece?" Hope whispered.

"From Pa. I just laugh and laugh when I think of his face when he discovered his poor slave—that's me—had gone off with the gold piece he loved so much."

"You stole—"

"He owed me."

"Shut your mouths. The burying ain't going to last all day." Zeke dropped the coin in his pocket and put the dirt back in the hole and replaced the rock and a few leaves. Then he took Jemima's hand and ran off through the cornfield.

John, who had said nothing, put his hand in Hope's and they followed. When Hope's side was beginning to cramp and John was falling behind, they arrived at another road.

"Take off those Shaker scarves," Zeke said to the girls.

Jemima threw hers to the ground and stepped over it. "Stupid," Zeke muttered as he went back and picked it up, folded it into a small square and put it in his pocket. "You want them to find it here? Take off your Shaker hat, John. And walk like we're on an outing, maybe going to visit someone."

As they walked along, Hope looked down at John. "You've grown," she said. "You're some taller and a lot fatter. They been treating you fine?"

He nodded. "Yea. Elder Grove said I was to drink two glasses of milk at every meal until I got fattened up. He almost promised to send me to the woodworking shop when school was out, but he didn't. I thought maybe he'd forgotten me. But today Zeke said Elder Grove wanted me to meet you here. Wasn't that nice?" He didn't wait for an answer. "Were you surprised when we jumped out of the tree? Funny, wasn't it? Wait till I tell Calvin. That's Calvin Fairchild. He's my best friend. We've been working together, hoeing in the garden."

"Hurry up," Zeke commanded.

Hope was confused. What was John talking about? Elder Grove wouldn't have given him permission to meet his sister. And he was planning to tell a boy named Calvin about jumping out of the tree. Did he think he would be returning to the boys' house?

John sneezed and then he grinned and trotted on after Zeke and Jemima. Hope followed.

No one passed them on the road. The first farmhouse they came to was a shack. The next was a large spread, like Uncle Josiah's. They turned into the lane.

The yard was deserted. No one came out of the house as they walked past it to a small barn. Beyond was a large barn. The small barn was empty except for several cats. Zeke climbed the ladder to the hayloft. The other three followed.

"We'll just make us a little nest here near the window where we can look out and enjoy the breezes." Zeke began to push the hay aside. "You make a nest over there," he said to Hope.

"Where are we?" Hope asked. "Why are we settling in? You didn't say anything about settling in, Jemima. I thought we were going directly into Pittsfield."

"You didn't ask. You were so busy worrying about your precious brother. 'I can't go without John,' you kept saying. John this, John that."

That was true. Jemima had told Hope her plan yesterday afternoon. She and Zeke had already worked everything out. The only question was John and Hope. After supper, Jemima had raised her hands over her head when she rose from the table. That was the signal that Zeke was to bring John when he came to meet her. It had seemed so simple then. It wasn't until later that Hope had begun to worry.

"You want to know where we are?"

Jemima laughed, dug around in the hay at the top of the ladder and pulled out a tin box painted with yellow roses. "Guess," she said.

"I guess this is Fay's farm. At least that's her lunch box. But why?"

"I told you, Hope. Me and Zeke had it all planned. We're going to stay here till it's dark and then we're going to head on out." She opened the box. "Must be about dinner time. See what I got for us. Yesterday after lunch, I just moved the food from one box to another. Told Fay to put her box up here when she got home." She handed them each a thick slice of cheese, two slices of dark bread, and a piece of apple pie.

"Oh Jemima, that's the food the little girls were supposed to take home with them. I think the kitchen sisters mean to give us more than we can eat so that there will be something for them to take home."

"So they're sharing with us just this once. Won't hurt 'em."

"Where's Fay and her family?" Hope was beginning to feel uneasy.

"Visiting in Stockbridge, for a wedding. We were lucky about one thing, that old Sister Bessie decided to die on Friday so she could be buried on Saturday—and not just any Saturday, but a Saturday when Fay's family was going visiting. Won't be no one here except the hired man. We'll have to be right quiet when he comes to milk the cows in the big barn."

"Stop your chattering and come over here, woman." Zeke scowled.

Jemima giggled. "You settle in, Hope. Take a nap. We have a long way to walk tonight, all the way to Pittsfield."

"Yeah," Zeke said. "We gotta get to Boston just as fast as we can. Remember that. We gotta get to Boston."

Jemima hadn't said anything about Boston. Hope wanted to go to Uncle Josiah's in Pittsfield. She flopped down beside John.

"Why are we here, Hope?" John sneezed. "Why do we have to hide when the hired man comes to milk the cows?"

"Because we are running away. To find Pa. So we can all be together."

"I didn't say good-bye to Calvin and Elder Grove. I can't just—" John sneezed again.

Don't let him start wheezing, Hope said to herself. Please, God, don't let him get sick. "I have something important to tell you, Johnny. Sister Lucy Jane, she's the teacher of the girls' school, she says that the body is just a sort of covering for the spirit. The body's the part they bury when someone dies. But the spirit of the person escapes. I think Ma's spirit is up there someplace flying around with Grandma and Grandpa—"

"Do you think that's true?"

"Yes," Hope said, wanting to believe what she was saying.

"Do you think Pa is up there with her?" John asked.

Hope stared at John. "Why would you think such a thing? Pa is big and strong. Pa's not dead. He couldn't be. Not Pa. Maybe he's in California, but most likely he's somewhere near, looking for us, or he will be soon. We'll go to Uncle Josiah and ask if he's had a letter from Pa Then maybe we'll go see the parson. Maybe we'll go on out to California ourselves. After we talk to the parson we can decide which is the best plan." She divided one of the slices of bread and gave half of it and some of the cheese to John. She ate the other half herself.

She could not see Jemima and Zeke in their nest at the other side of the hayloft but she heard a whispering murmur punctuated by Jemima's giggles.

"Could we go to California by ourselves, Hope? We don't have any money. Pa went part of the way on the train. Remember? He bought a ticket to take him halfway across the country."

"I remember. We'd have to earn some money. I could work for some rich lady in her kitchen."

"And I could feed the chickens. I don't like to scoop manure but I know how to do it. And milk. I know how to milk."

"It might take us until next spring to earn enough. Pa might come for us before then—"

"Quick," Zeke hissed. "Bury yourselves in the hay." Hope and John lay flat and pulled hay down over themselves. At the same time, they heard the clop-clop of horses' hooves in the lane leading from the road to the barn. Then footsteps in front of the barn.

"No one home at the house, Brother!" one man shouted. "Saturday. Must have gone to town or visiting."

The footsteps entered the barn; one set climbed the ladder. John began to tremble and sniff. He was doing his best to hold a sneeze.

"No one here," the man called from the top of the ladder. He continued talking as he climbed back down. "Where to now?"

"Too bad no one noticed they were gone until we were sitting down for our noontime meal. If they got a ride, they could be miles from here by now. Better check the train station."

Footsteps away from the barn and among the farm buildings were, at last, followed by the snort of a horse and then the sound of hooves. When the visitors were near the road, John sneezed mightily.

Hope pushed the hay away from him and hugged him. "That was good, the way you held that sneeze," she whispered. "Isn't it nice to be together again after such a long, long time?"

"Yea."

"Why do you say yea? You're not a Shaker."

"Nay. I mean, no."

"I hate living with the Shakers, John. Surely you do too."

"The food is good. And the round barn is amazing. And the teaching brother gave me peppermints when I gave the right answers. And Calvin is my friend. And—"

"And in all these months we were never allowed to talk to each other, not even once. And there are rules for almost everything, even how you hold your hands in your lap." Hope wanted to shake John. Instead she took a deep breath and told him about California, where it never snows and where the ocean stretches all the way to China. She lay back in the hay and relaxed. John lay with his head on her shoulder. It was nice to have him close.

She awoke in darkness to the sound of John wheezing. He coughed, the dry hacking cough that terrified her; soon he would be fighting for every breath. His lips might turn blue. He wouldn't be able to speak or to move until the attack ended—if it ended. She had heard of children who died of asthma. Above the coughing, she heard whispers.

"We can't just leave them," Jemima hissed.

"You didn't really think we'd take them with us?" Zeke sounded surprised.

"But I told Hope she could go with us to her uncle's farm. She's my friend."

"And her little brother? Listen to him. Heard him do that a couple of nights in the boys' house. Everybody'd gather round and give him medicine and put poultices on his chest and fuss over him. Elder Grove thought it was hay that did it. 'Don't let him pitch the hay down to the cows,' he said. Elder Grove treats him like he was an angel sent from heaven."

"But they only want to go to Pittsfield..."

"They've had what they wanted, a whole afternoon together. Isn't our fault they slept through most of it. Your friend wanted to see her precious brother. So she's seen him. If they want to go to Pittsfield, they can go in the morning, by themselves. Come, my Jemima. Come..."

Think fast, Hope commanded herself. She stood up in the black loft and climbed blindly over the hay toward the voices.

"Please, Zeke, Jemima. Don't go off without us. Wherever you're going—"

"Boston. Don't forget. We're going to Boston." Zeke was angry. "And you are not going with us."

"Then help me get John back to the Shakers. He can't walk when he's having trouble breathing. Just through the cornfield to the road. I could get him the rest of the way or get someone to come for him. Please."

"You'll be all right. Stay here till morning, then go get someone to help you. I've seen John like this before. All he needs is a little rest."

Just minutes earlier, Zeke had told Jemima about the medicines and the poultices the brothers had used to help John when he was sick. Now he said John didn't need anything but rest. Zeke was a wicked liar!

"Please, Jemima," Hope begged. "Stay with us. Or help me get John back to the Shakers. We don't even have water."

"You can have the rest of ours."

Hope heard her moving across the hay and then she felt the pail by her side and a pat on her arm.

"Good-bye, Hope," she said. "You were always bellyaching about seeing your precious brother. You talked about him almost as much as that stupid Eunice talked about Mother

Ann. You can thank me for a whole afternoon and night with your brother. He'll be fine in the morning, and then you can go on to your uncle's. It'll be easier to travel in the day, anyway. I'm coming, Zeke."

Hope listened, sorrowing, to the footsteps on the ladder and across the barn—and to John wheezing.

"Why didn't you tell me that hay makes you wheeze?" she asked.

John couldn't answer as he fought for his next breath.

Hope crawled on across the loft to where Jemima and Zeke had made their nest in front of a window without glass. A few stars and a sliver of a moon lightened the sky to dark gray. Hope pushed the hay back away from the window and swept the rough floorboards with her hand, picking up a painful splinter, which she was unable to suck out of her finger.

She crawled back over the hay to John. "You can't stay lying in this hay, Johnny, if it's hay that makes you sick. It's too cold to spend the night outside. So I've made a nice place for you, over by the window. Come on, Johnny. Stand up and lean on me. You'll be much better over by the window. In the morning we'll do whatever you want. We'll go back to the Shakers or we'll go on to Uncle

Josiah's or the parson's. Whatever you want."

While she spoke she hauled John to his feet and dragged him across the hay to the clearing. She closed the shutter over the window to keep out the cool night air. How far into the night were they? The hired man must have come to milk the cows in the big barn while she slept. She ate half of the last piece of bread and set the rest aside for John. He couldn't stop coughing long enough to eat now.

She sat with her back against the wall and pulled John to a sitting position in front of her. She rubbed his back and then she rested his head against her shoulder.

Hour after hour John coughed and wheezed and gasped for breath. Hope alternately rubbed his back and pulled him close. As the night wore on, her sorrow deepened. She tried not to let herself think about children who died of asthma.

As her sorrow increased, so did her anger. She was mad at Pa. Why hadn't he come for them? He'd left her to take care of Ma and now John. It wasn't fair. Hope wanted to leave the silly Shakers, but she couldn't get away now. That was John's fault. In the morning she'd have to beg the Church family to take both of them back. Most of all, she was mad at Jemima and Zeke.

She wondered about the herbs and the poultices the Shaker brothers used to ease John's coughing and wheezing. She thought about going back for help, but she couldn't find her way in the dark. Besides, John would be frightened if she left him, and that would make his chest even tighter.

Hope had to try to keep her brother calm, and so she told him again about the spirits being welcomed by their friends and carried off to heaven. That was a happy story. And then she told him about the baby Jesus and the shepherds and the wise men. She told him about Noah and the ark he filled with animals of every sort.

The first time John was silent, she thought he was listening to her story—until his body turned stiff and he threw his head into her shoulder. She pounded on his back, and at last he shuddered and drew a breath into his body.

Would the night never end?

5

Dawn crept in so softly that Hope didn't notice until she heard a rooster crow. John's cough was still constant but shallower and quieter. Perhaps the attack was ending. She opened the shutter to let in the gray light—and gasped when she looked back at John. His lips were blue. And so were his fingertips.

"I have to go for help," she said aloud. Please don't die, she begged silently. "I'll run as fast as I can, and if I see anyone along the way, I'll make them help me."

He blinked his eyes so that she knew he heard her, but he was too sick to speak. She scooted her body away from him and propped him up against the wall. He slumped like a doll that had lost its stuffing.

She slid down the ladder and began to run through the barn, down the lane to the road, down the road toward the cornfield. Pain pierced her side, but she kept running. At last she had to slow down.

Should she cut through the cornfield or stay on the road? She was trying to decide while she clutched her sides and struggled for breath. Finally she straightened her back and prepared to run through the field. But first she looked back. A wagon was approaching. When she recognized it as one of the wagons the brothers used when they went out into the world, a weight lifted from her chest. She ran down the middle of the road toward it, waving her hands and shouting to the two brothers on the high seat.

Before they had come to a stop she tried to climb up beside the brother who was driving. He barred her way with a stiff arm. "What can we do for you?" he asked.

"I'm the sister of John Douglas. Do you know him?"

"Yea. We've been out all night looking for him—and you."

"He's sick. In a barn back there. The first big farm. Let me show you."

"Nay. We'll find him ourselves. We thought we looked in all the barns. Which one?"

"The loft of the first, smaller one."

"The horse barn." He clucked to the horse.

"Let me go with you," she cried, but the horse was already trotting back toward Fay's farm.

For a moment she stood in the middle of the road and shook her fist at the backs of the brothers. She hated them and their silly rules that kept her from John even when he needed her most. Tears began to wash her face. She turned and walked back toward the barn. She had to see John.

Hope stood at the end of the lane and watched as one of the brothers carried John out of the barn. He was wrapped in a heavy blanket—she was glad of that. The brother lifted him up to the other brother, who was waiting in the bed of the wagon. Then the brother who had carried John from the barn climbed up onto the wagon seat. The horse trotted down the lane, seeming to gather speed as it approached Hope.

"Go back through the cornfield," the driver shouted to Hope as the wagon sped past her.

What else could she do? She turned back and walked slowly down the road, so tired she could hardly stand upright. Tears continued to trickle down her face. When she got to the cornfield, she wanted to sit and rest but she didn't, afraid that she would not have the strength to get up again.

She was stumbling between furrows when she heard a high, reedy voice calling her name.

"Here," she sobbed and began to cry harder.

Within minutes she was walking between Sister Anna and another sister whom Hope did not know. Neither of them spoke, but they held her elbows gently and guided her back to the row of trees and bushes and along it until they reached the meeting house, where they crossed the road.

On the second floor of the brick dwelling, a washtub was filled with warm water. Sister Anna washed Hope's hair then turned away while Hope washed her own body.

When she was wrapped in a heavy towel, Sister Anna began to comb the snarls out of her wet hair. Suddenly she dropped the comb and lifted Hope's hand. "What's this?" Those were the first words she had spoken to Hope.

This was Hope's finger, which was red and swollen to twice its usual size. It began to throb, and she remembered that it had hurt during the night. "I got a splinter," she said. "I think it's still in there."

Sister Anna nodded and picked up the comb. The other sister brought a soft nightgown and dropped it over Hope's head. She wanted to protest, to tell them that she had to get dressed so that she could go to see John. She couldn't sleep until she had seen him.

They led her to another room on the second floor. Along one wall were rows of small drawers and shelves with colored bottles.

"Welcome to the infirmary," laughed a plump little old lady. "I'm Sister Chloe Slosson, the nurse. I hear you've had an adventure."

Sister Anna lifted Hope's hand to show the old lady the swollen finger. "She says she picked up a splinter."

Sister Chloe made a few clucking noises while she pushed Hope down into a chair and stretched Hope's arm across a table next to it. Then she put on a pair of spectacles, examined the finger, and rubbed something on it that made it tingle. "Don't look," she said.

Hope stared at Sister Chloe's wrinkled cheek and the wen near the outside corner of her eye. The little ball of flesh bobbled as the nurse pricked and squeezed Hope's finger. Hope wondered if the wen was hard like a raw pea, or soft like a cooked one.

"Look at that," Sister Chloe said, pointing to the sliver on the palm of her hand. "We'll send it out to the brethren. It's so big they can use it to prop up the old sheep shed." She laughed heartily at her joke as she dabbed a cloth at the drops of blood on Hope's finger and then rubbed a salve into it. "Good as new by the time you wake up," she said.

Sister Anna set a tray on the table. On it was a dish of hot milk with a piece of bread in it and nutmeg floating on top.

Hope ate it quickly. "Now I've got to get dressed and go see my brother," she said.

"Not now. Now you are going to sleep."

Terror invaded Hope's brain. "If you are the nurse, why aren't you taking care of my brother? He needs you." She thought of his blue lips. His body hadn't moved while he was being carried from the barn. They wouldn't let her into the wagon to see him. "Is he …? He can't be …?" She couldn't speak the word *dead.*

Sister Chloe patted her arm. "Nay, Hope. Elder Grove has sent word that John is very weak but he is breathing much better."

"And his lips? Are they blue?"

"I'm sure his color is returning."

"I want to see him."

"That will be up to the elders. Perhaps in a day or two—"

"I want to see him now. He's my brother. I've taken care of him all his life. I promised our mother …" She sounded like a cranky child and she knew it. "I'm sorry. I am thankful to the brothers for caring for him," she whispered.

Sister Chloe took her hand and led her to a bed in the corner of the next room. As she sank down into it, she noticed that another sister, even older than Sister Chloe, had rolled up to the bed in a chair that had wheels on it.

"Sleep, my child," the old woman said, and then she began to hum a tune.

The western sun was streaming into the windows when Hope awoke. The old lady was sitting beside her, still or again. When their eyes met, the old lady smiled broadly. She had six teeth in her mouth, four on top and two on the bottom. She was almost as small as Catherine, and her face was lined with wrinkles. She looked merry, like an elf.

"Did you rest well, my child?" she asked. "Are you hungry?"

"Yes." Hope yawned. "Thank you."

"Jump up and help yourself to the food on the plate over there. You missed dinner but, as I told Sister Chloe, Sunday dinner is easy to miss."

Sunday? Of course it was Sunday. The funeral had been on Saturday. Already that seemed a long time ago. The plate held the usual Sunday dinner: baked beans, applesauce, and bread. The Shakers only did work that was absolutely necessary on Sunday, like feeding the livestock and milking the cows. They did not cook. The beans had been started on Saturday and had cooked all night without attention. Even cold, they were delicious.

The old sister rolled her chair near Hope. "I'm Sister Hannah," she said. "I was born the year our country was born, 1776. When I was a little girl, I saw Mother Ann in the flesh."

"I'm pleased to meet you," Hope said. "Did I keep you from the meeting? I'm sorry."

Sister Hannah held up her hand to protest. "I'm sure the brothers were glad not to have to carry me and my chair down the stairs."

"The brothers come to this side of the building? They carry you? How can that be?" It was against the rules for a Shaker man to touch a Shaker woman, or any woman.

"Actually, I roll my chair to their side of the building. I don't weigh much more than a banty hen these days, but it's easier for the men to carry me than it would be for the women. When you get to be an old lady, they may even let you see your brother when he is sick." Her laugh was like a soft cackle.

John! Suddenly Hope pictured him lying limp in the loft, his lips and fingers blue. "What have you heard about John? Is he better?"

"Yea, Hope. Sister Chloe asked me to tell you that the brethren gave him coltsfoot, henbane, and horehound, and he's breathing normal now. They're going to start giving him lobelia on a regular basis for a while. I expect they also gave him a mustard plaster."

"Did she say when I can see him?"

Sister Hannah shook her head. "Nay, child. Take the advice of an old lady and don't pester the sisters. Best if you be a little mouse, hiding in a hole for a few days."

Hope was confused. Why should she hide? And then she understood. "They're angry because I tried to run away."

"Yea. And you took your little brother with you."

"I didn't mean for him to be sick. I didn't know that hay makes him sick." Hope wondered about Jemima and Zeke. Had they been brought back, too? She didn't ask. "I'm sorry I caused so much trouble. Will I be punished?"

"That's not for me to say, child. Definitely not on the Sabbath. Tomorrow? Perhaps. Sister Anna said that you were not to get dressed or leave this room. But she said you could read to me, if you feel up to it. Do you? I'd like the psalm that begins, 'I will lift up mine eyes unto the hills.' "

" 'From whence cometh my help.' " Hope finished the line while she took the Bible from Sister Hannah and searched for the psalm. " 'My help cometh from the Lord which made heaven and earth ...' "

Hope read until she was hoarse, and then

Sister Hannah taught her a song called "In Yonder's Valley."

Sister Chloe brought their suppers to them. She was as wrinkled as Sister Hannah, but she was inches broader. She didn't walk; she scurried like a chipmunk. She told Hope that she was to stay in the room for the night.

"May I go to school tomorrow?" Hope asked.

Sister Chloe shook her head vigorously so that the wen beneath her eye bobbled. "Sister Anna said she will bring your breakfast here—and a dress. You are to be ready when she comes for you."

"When will that be?"

"I don't know. No more questions, please."

When Sister Chloe left the room, Hope turned to Sister Hannah. "What's going to happen to me?" she asked the old lady.

"I can't remember when a girl ran away and was brought back. I wouldn't worry too much."

"But you would worry some?"

Sister Hannah smiled, but she did not answer.

When the first bell rang at four thirty the next morning, Hope was already awake. She jumped out of bed and washed her face and braided her hair neatly. She and Sister Chloe lifted Sister Hannah out of bed. She had been right when she said she didn't weigh much more than a banty hen. They helped her wash and dress. Hope brushed her thin wisps of hair and arranged her crisp white cap.

Sister Hannah wasn't able to leave the room to go to the privy and Hope wasn't allowed to leave. They had both used a commode in the room. It was odorless. "Because it is vented through the wall into the chimney," Sister Hannah explained. "The fumes are carried away like smoke. Aren't our sisters and brothers clever people? We have so many good ideas."

Hope nodded, agreeing. There were the little stoves that kept whole rooms warm, and all kinds of special laundry equipment. She'd been told that a Shaker invented the flat broom and the circular saw. Some Shakers were very clever.

Sister Anna brought them their breakfasts and a dark blue summer dress for Hope. It was not new but it was not one she had worn before. Sister Anna also brought a new white scarf. The dress fit well, and Hope arranged the scarf carefully. She had left her old scarf in the loft to protect John's head from the splintery boards. Perhaps the brothers had brought it back.

She walked to the window and stared

down at the grass, which was dotted with beads of dew. She watched the girls walk, two by two, from the dwelling toward the schoolhouse across the road. Hope walked around the room and back to the window. She wiggled her fingers and her toes. She hunched and dropped her shoulders. Yesterday the room had seemed cozy. Today, although the door to the hall was wide open, it felt like a prison. She walked back and forth, back and forth, wondering what would happen to her. Would the Shakers send her back to Uncle Josiah? Is that what they were waiting for? For Uncle Josiah to come for her? She had heard that the Shakers did not beat their animals—or their children. But Hope's sin was huge.

"You're wearing out the floor, child," Sister Hannah said. "Come and get to work. We will hem towels. Sit here."

Hope sat and took the cloth the old lady handed her. She turned up the edge of the cloth and jabbed the needle into it.

"Slowly, carefully," Sister Hannah said.

"It's a towel, Sister Hannah. Just a towel. I know that the cloth will unravel if it is not hemmed, but any kind of hem will do. Who looks at the hem of a towel?"

"Mother Ann said, 'Do all your work as though you had a thousand years to live on earth, and as you would if you knew you must die tomorrow.' Notice that Mother said 'all your work,' not all your work that people will see."

Mother Ann's opinion on the subject of towels was of no interest to Hope, but she said nothing while she concentrated on stitches worthy of a ball gown.

At last Sister Anna knocked on the wall beside the open door, entered the room, and took the towel from Hope. "Well done," she said. "Now smooth your hair and come with me. Quickly. You are expected at the ministry."

"The ministry?" Hope's knees suddenly felt like noodles. The ministry elders and eldresses were in charge of all of the families at Hancock and at two other Shaker villages. They concentrated on serious matters; everyday problems were solved by the family elders and eldresses and by trustees and deacons and caretakers.

"Hurry," Sister Anna hissed as they rushed down the stairs, out the door, and across the road.

Through open doors, Hope saw that there were workshops on the first floor of the ministry—every Shaker did manual labor, even the elders and eldresses. They hurried up the stairs, and Sister Anna knocked beside an open door and pushed Hope forward.

"Stand there," she said, pointing to a spot in the middle of the floor.

Two women sat in straight chairs with a table between them. Both of them smiled. Eldress Cassandana Brewster spoke. "Thank you, Sister Anna. You are Hope Douglas?"

"Yes, ma'am."

"I understand that while we were burying our dear sister on Saturday, you and Jemima Jones ran off with Ezekiel Foley and your brother, John Douglas. Is that true?"

"Yes, ma'am."

"Why?"

"I wanted to see my brother and—" She stopped midsentence. It would not be wise to tell these women that she hated their village and their rules.

"Have you been ill treated here?"

"No, ma'am."

"Have you been unhappy?"

"I miss my brother—and my father. We expected him to come for us, but we haven't even had a letter from him. Something is wrong. I must find out what."

"Your uncle told us that no one had heard from your father since he left for California more than a year ago. I understand that you are a bright girl. Surely you did not think that you could just walk out of here and find your way to California. If you did try that, you would not be behaving intelligently, would you?"

"No, ma'am. But he might have come back to Pittsfield and not known where to find us."

"Surely your uncle would have told him that you were here with us. He would have sent any letters here. You know that you risked your little brother's life, taking him away as you did. Was that intelligent—or loving?"

"No, ma'am. I am especially sorry about that." Hope lifted her head, determined not to cry.

"What about Jemima? Do you blame her?"

"No. I could have refused to go. I wish I had."

"Good. Do you know where she and that young man went?"

Hope thought for a moment. They hadn't said not to tell. "They said they were going to Boston."

"Which probably means that they were going anyplace but Boston."

Hope hadn't thought of that. "Are you looking for them?" she asked.

"No longer. Ezekiel broke the terms of his apprenticeship, but he was too worldly and too devious to become an acceptable Shaker.

We had hoped to tame Jemima, but it is too late now for that. It is not too late for you and your brother. Elder Grove tells me that he is a lovely, gentle child. Do you agree?"

"Yes. Our mother said that John was born with a sweet nature."

"I understand that you are spirited but kind as well as bright—and a capable worker. I want you to promise to stay with us."

"But our father will come..."

"If your father comes for you or sends for you and you want to be with him, we will release you. When you become an adult you may choose for yourself—to become a full Shaker or to leave. We, of course, hope you will become one of us. In the meantime, will you promise not to leave the village without permission?"

Hope said nothing. It wasn't a promise she wanted to make, but what else could she do? "I promise," she said, at last.

"Good. Now go to school. After school you will go directly to Sister Hannah. She will teach you to knit and you will read to her. Then you will go to the kitchen and pick up two supper plates. You and Sister Hannah will eat together upstairs. You will observe the rule of silence during the meal and you will pray before and after you eat. Then you will take your dishes to the kitchen and go to your room on the third floor and participate in our regular evening activities. You will do this every weekday until the school term ends. You may go now."

Was that it? Her punishment was to spend a few hours every day with Sister Hannah? "Thank you," she said, trying not to smile. And then she paused. "Please, ma'am. May I see my brother?"

The eldress shook her head. "Nay, child. He is being nursed by the brethren. I will ask one of the elders to let him know that you are concerned about him and that you have promised to stay with us."

"Until our father comes."

Eldress Dana looked into Hope's eyes and smiled broadly. "Fear not. John will not forget your love for him. In the meantime, he is loved by all of us. So, too, are you, our dear Hope. This is a place where love abides. The blessings of Father God and Mother Wisdom go with you."

"Thank you," Hope whispered, and lowered her head while she blinked back tears.

As she entered the schoolroom, Sister Lucy Jane welcomed her with a nod and a smile. Hope took her seat and looked around. She felt as if she had been away for a very long time. Yet everything looked the same except that Jemima's place was empty, and so was Fay's.

The two little sisters looked no hungrier than usual. Did Sister Lucy Jane know that Jemima had stolen the food meant for their family? Hope wasn't sorry that she had given their food to John but she was sorry she had eaten it herself. She could have gone without food for a few hours.

When it was time for dinner, Hope ate only part of hers. She slipped the bread spread with peach butter and a piece of cheese into the box the little girls carried back and forth with them.

"I'm glad you're back," Catherine said when the girls went outside for their midday exercise.

"We all worried about you," Eunice cooed. "The sisters were so upset. Weren't they, Rachel?"

"The sisters were so upset," Rachel repeated.

Eunice looked at Hope as if she expected her to speak. Instead Hope turned away. She couldn't stand the sight of Miss Piety's sour face and stringy hair.

Eunice was not to be ignored. She put her hand on Hope's shoulder to hold her back and spoke loudly for all the girls to hear. "I prayed for you, of course. And I suggested that the others do the same. I told the others that Jemima must have made you go. And Fay helped her. They are the instruments of Satan. But you, dear Hope, you must pray for strength, lest you be tempted again."

Hope put her hands over her ears but she could not shut out Eunice's voice, which reminded her of molasses, thick and syrupy.

"And you had to go before the ministry. None of the other girls have ever had to do that. Poor Hope. Don't you want to tell us about it?"

"Tell us about it," Rachel repeated, her big eyes bulging so that she looked like a cow.

Hope lowered her hands to her hips and turned to glare at Eunice while she gathered the words that would silence her.

Before she could speak them, Sister Lucy Jane came out of the schoolhouse. "Remember these words of Mother Ann: 'Let your words be few and seasoned with grace.'" She smiled at Hope.

Why, Hope asked herself crossly, were the sisters being so kind? And why did their kindness make her feel so uncomfortable? She wished they had given her a tongue-lashing followed by a beating so that she could have gone on hating all of them, not just Eunice.

6

John sat on a bench near the door to the boys' house. He leaned his head back against the wood siding. The house was empty; the caretakers and the boys, except John, were out working. Calvin said they had spent the morning weeding and thinning the young beet plants. Others were hoeing the weeds from between the rows of corn. Two of the older boys and some of the brethren had cleaned out one of the smaller barns. They'd be whitewashing it now.

An old man came to the door of the brethren's shop across the path. In one hand he held an oval box; with the other hand he waved to John. Then he turned and went back inside. He was too old to work in the fields and spent his days making wooden boxes. One of the caretakers had asked him to keep an eye on "the invalid." That's what Calvin had been calling John—the invalid.

John hadn't done any work in the ten days since he had gone off to meet Hope. He spent almost a week in bed. Now he felt fine when he woke up. Before noon, however, he was tired. Even today the walk back from the brick dwelling after dinner had seemed miles long. He'd had to use the handrail to pull himself up the steep stairs to the room he shared with Calvin and two other boys. He couldn't remember dropping his head on the pillow. He had been coughing and sniffing when he awoke—he always coughed and sniffed when he woke. Otherwise he felt fine except that he was afraid he had slept too long.

He'd run down the stairs and out to the road. The windows of the schoolhouse were still open, which meant that the school day was not yet over. So he'd gone back to his bench to wait in the sun. Already his coughing and sniffing had stopped.

Brother Harry had said that Hope was concerned about him. He was concerned about her. He couldn't figure out why she had wanted to run away. They couldn't go to California on their own. Most likely they would never see Pa again. Pa would have come for them if he could. He hadn't come; therefore he must be dead.

John had been foolish, too. Like he told Elder Grove, he just never thought that Zeke might be lying to him. Even after they got to the barn and he began wheezing, John could have left. Hope would have been cross, but she would probably have come back with him.

Elder Grove said that John had to learn to do his own thinking and not let Hope or anyone else think for him. John grinned to himself. Elder Grove wanted John to think for himself as long as what he thought was what the Shakers wanted him to think. Most people were like that.

He couldn't remember much about the night in the barn except that there were times when he thought he had already breathed his last breath. He didn't remember that Hope had left him to get help or that the brothers had carried him out of the barn and brought him home in a wagon. He did remember the smell of the ointment they rubbed on his chest and the taste of the medicine they made him drink and the heat of the poultice on his chest.

From across the road came the sound of footsteps. John rose from the bench and walked to the fence. He stood leaning against it watching the girls as they came out of the schoolhouse and marched along on the other side of the road. At the head of the line was a sister holding the hand of the smallest child. At the back of the line was Hope. He wanted to shout to her, or at least wave, but that was forbidden. So he stood tall and hoped she would look in his direction.

She was almost opposite him when she turned her head. He stood as tall and straight as possible so that she could see that he was well. Her face did not change. Was it possible that she did not see him? And then she lowered her head slightly in his direction. I see you, John, she was saying in a quiet Shaker way.

He lifted one finger. The brethren took good care of me, Hope. You don't have to be concerned any longer.

He turned back and entered the brethren's shop. "Could I help you?" he asked the box maker.

The old man studied his face and asked him how he felt and then gave him a wooden handle to sand and make smooth. "Do it outside, away from the dust. We don't want more wheezing from you."

John sat on his bench and smoothed the wood until it felt like butter.

When Sister Hannah had waved to Hope from the window, she rolled her chair over to the door to be ready to greet her as she entered the room. "You look happy, child," she said.

Hope nodded and wheeled the old lady back to the place she liked best in front of one of the large windows. She lifted a chair from two pegs and set it near the wheeled chair.

When she had seated herself, she grinned

at Sister Hannah and leaned close to her and spoke in a low voice. "I saw my brother. He was standing by the fence on the other side of the road. On purpose, I think, so I could see that he is well. He can't be strong yet or he would be working in the fields with the other boys. Some of them are hoeing the corn in the field just beyond the schoolhouse. But he was standing tall and he looked healthy."

"That's good news, Hope. You didn't speak to him?"

"I didn't even wave."

"Good girl."

"I just nodded my head the tiniest bit so he'd know I saw him and he raised one finger just the tiniest bit so I know that he knew that I saw him."

"Good."

"Did you ever have a brother or a sister?"

"Of course. I have tens of each. You know that."

"I mean a flesh-and-blood brother or sister."

"Yea. You have met my flesh-and-blood sister, Josephine. She said you knead bread with great skill."

"She's your real sister? You have others? How do you happen to be here?"

"We are here through the grace of Father God and Mother Wisdom. When I was seven years old, we gave our hearts to the

Believers. My mother, my father, two brothers, and Josephine and me. Even our hired man came with us, but he didn't stay long."

"Your hired man? Where did you live?"

"The cornfield you just mentioned belonged to my father and his father before him. Our house was on the corner right by the road. Years ago they moved the house to the Second family. It's still there, I understand."

"Why? Did you have some bad years? Were you poor?"

Sister Hannah laughed merrily. "Nay. We heard Mother Ann herself speak. My mother and father talked about what they heard for months. They discussed it with others. My mother said that the hardest part was not giving up the farm and their goods and money. It was giving up one another."

"What do you mean?"

"My parents could not be together once they became Shakers. After they joined, my little brother got sick and my mother had to let others nurse him until he died. That was very hard. But they believed, as I believe, and as Josephine believes. My greatest joy is knowing that soon my spirit will leave this stiff, achy body and soar upward to join the heavenly spirits."

"Where is your other brother?"

"When he grew up, he decided that this

life was not for him. He left and headed West. He came back for a visit once—about twenty years ago. He is a blacksmith in Ohio and has five children."

"Was he angry about your pa giving the farm away?"

"I don't know. I didn't ask. He had no right to be upset. I was glad to see him but I was sad, too, because, you see, his spirit will not join ours."

"Why not?"

"Because he spurned the Shaker way. He said he was a Methodist."

"Don't Methodists go to heaven?"

"I don't know, Hope. Maybe there is another heaven for Methodists."

"My ma said that people who are good go to heaven. Doesn't matter what church you go to." Hope was feeling uneasy. "My mother was good. Her spirit must have flown up to the heaven for good people."

Sister Hannah said nothing for a bit. Then she smiled at Hope. "It's too hot to knit, so why don't you just read to me while I finish the hem on this sheet?"

School days were all alike. Hope rose with the bell at four-thirty and helped air beds and sweep floors. After breakfast she went to school. She spent the late afternoon with

Sister Hannah. In the evening she went to the meeting downstairs and then she went to bed.

Saturdays and Sundays she was not required to sit with Sister Hannah. Saturdays Hope usually worked in the kitchen. On the Sabbath two of the brothers carried Sister Hannah down the stairs. Another brother carried her chair so that she could be wheeled across the road to the meeting house. The old lady ate in the dining room and sat in one of the downstairs rooms with Sister Josephine and some of the other old sisters. After the afternoon family meeting, the brothers carried her back up to the second floor.

Sundays seemed longer and sadder than the other days of the week. The service in the meeting house was tiresome. Many of the songs were jolly and some were beautiful, but the singers were not allowed to harmonize. They had no musical instruments. Hope hated the dancing, especially when it became frenzied.

Sunday dinner was simple. Sunday afternoons were dismal; Hope wished she could have spent them with Sister Hannah. Even during the hot summer, girls had to stay in their third-floor rooms in the dwelling. They were expected to converse quietly or read from the Bible or other sacred writings. With Jemima gone, Hope had no one she wanted to talk with.

If only she had a novel to read, but novels were another forbidden pleasure. Some afternoons she tried to remember the stories by Nathaniel Hawthorne in his *Twice Told Tales.* She made up details she couldn't remember. She flexed her leg muscles and thought about the pleasure of walking miles, alone.

She also thought about Pa. Unless he came for her and John, she would spend all the years until she grew up in this Shaker prison. She continued to pray for him every time she knelt in the dining room—and every Sunday afternoon.

The days went on, one after another, in the established pattern—until the second day in July. On that day, the older girls were excused from school to help pick strawberries. The berries were fully ripe and deliciously sweet. The first ones went into Hope's mouth.

Although strawberries do not have thorns like raspberries and blackberries, they are difficult to pick because they grow close to the ground. Within an hour, Hope's back was beginning to hurt. Still it was pleasant to be out in the sunshine eating and picking.

Last year Hope and John had picked berries together. Pa had already been gone for four months. Ma's sickness was beginning, but she had loved the berries. They hadn't had enough sugar to make jam so they had eaten all they picked.

Now Pa has been gone for one year and four months. Hope said that sentence over and over to herself. Her hands slowed to a stop. Was Pa never coming back? Surely he would have come back, or sent for them, or written to them, if he were able. What if he were not able? What if he were dead?

That night in Fay's barn, John had suggested that Pa might be dead, but Hope had closed her mind. Pa had to be alive and traveling toward them. She popped a strawberry in her mouth and rushed to pick as many berries as possible in the shortest time possible. She thought about the strawberry jam and strawberry pie the sisters would make. But the awful thought kept sneaking into her brain. What if Pa were dead? She picked strawberries as if each were her enemy.

By noon, the vines had been picked clean, except for a few berries that were not yet ripe.

"Did you pick all of those yourself?" Sister Anna asked when she saw Hope's basket. "You have picked more than any two of us. Look, sisters, Hope has put us all to shame."

The sisters all smiled at her.

"I could have picked a bushel of strawberries, too," Eunice whimpered, "if I had not been praying. Whenever I am on my knees, I pray. I can't help myself." She smiled her sugary smile.

Hope noticed that the sisters turned away from her silently, except for Sister Anna, who frowned and spoke sharply. "I remind you, Eunice, that Mother Ann was very specific in her instructions. She said: 'Hearts to God and hands to work.' In this case, our hands were expected to pick berries."

Eunice sniffed and bowed her head. Hope bowed her head, too, to hide the grin that was creeping across her face.

The girls went back to school for the afternoon, and then Hope went to sit with Sister Hannah.

"Greetings, my dear strawberry girl." The old sister's smile was bright. "I hear you picked more berries than anyone thought possible. We are all so pleased with you."

Hope wasn't surprised that Sister Hannah had heard about her accomplishment. The old lady knew everything that went on in her Shaker family. Several of the sisters had permission to visit her whenever they could spare a few minutes. Few of them came while Hope was on duty, but many of them came earlier in the day.

"How were you able to do that?" Sister Hannah asked.

Hope didn't say anything while she

thought about the answer. At last she spoke. "I was trying to keep a thought from catching up with me. It helped some to think only of strawberries and how fast I could work."

"Was the thought you were running from dreadful? Were you frightened? Should you tell Sister Anna or Sister Lucy Jane about it?"

Hope shook her head as she felt tears rising behind her eyes. She picked up her work and knit two rows before she dropped the stocking in her lap. "I haven't heard from my pa for a year and four months," she whispered. "I don't know why he hasn't come for us, or at least written us. He would if he could. I know that. Could he be dead, Sister Hannah? Do you think he is dead?"

"I don't know, my dear." She took Hope's hand in her little gnarled one and held it. Neither of them spoke for a long time.

Haying had begun on July 2 and continued on dry days throughout the month. All the brothers and the boys helped, except for the very old, the very young, and John. Elder Grove was convinced that hay caused John's asthma.

Even though he was forbidden to enter a hay field or work in a hayloft or even to look at hay, he continued to cough, especially in the morning.

"It's a puzzle," Brother Harry said. "Something else must enter your lungs to make

you cough in the morning. Every day you feel well enough, we want you to work along with the other boys—except when they are working with hay—until we figure out what it is."

The next week, John and three other boys were sent to clean out a chicken house. It was a nasty task, scooping manure, sweeping feathers from the walls, and replacing the straw in the boxes where the hens laid their eggs. They had hardly begun when John felt his chest begin to tighten. He hid a sneeze in his arm and swallowed coughs. Then he began to wheeze.

"That's one way of getting out of this job," the boy who was in charge of the work said with a sneer. "Just stop making that noise and get on with the work."

"Clean here by the door where you can get some fresh air," Calvin whispered as he changed places with John.

John couldn't answer until he leaned out of the doorway and filled his lungs with fresh air. Then he coughed, and coughed again and again. Between coughs he scooped manure into a wheelbarrow. His chest began to rattle.

"Look at him," Calvin said loudly. "He's sick."

"He's pretending to be sick," the older boy sneered.

"I'll do his work, if you'll—"

Brother Harry rushed into the chicken house, reached for John's hand, pulled him out into the yard, and set him down under a tree. "What kind of a brother are you?" he shouted back over his shoulder as he began to rub John's back. "This child is suffering, as anyone with eyes and ears could tell. You were in charge, Jacob. You finish that chicken house by yourself. Calvin and Christian, you can split wood until dinner. As for you, John, we now know why you cough in the morning. It's feathers, as in feather pillows. Go sit in the sun with old Brother Amos and let him tell you his stories."

Brother Amos was a feeble old man, nearing ninety, who greeted John warmly and started a story about his early days with the Shakers, but he fell asleep before he finished it. When he awoke, he started another story and again fell asleep before he finished it.

When John went up to his bed that night, he discovered that his soft fluffy pillow had been replaced by a hard lump in a pillow case.

He arose as usual at the sound of the four thirty bell the next morning. An hour and a half later, as they were walking to the brick dwelling for breakfast, Brother Harry asked him about his chest.

John stopped and turned to look up at Brother Harry. "I never thought about my chest," he said. "I've scooped oats for the horses and scattered corn for the chickens—I didn't get close to them—and I haven't coughed once."

"Puzzle solved. Feathers make you sick. How'd you like the pillow I found for you? Almost as hard as a block of wood, isn't it?"

"But it didn't make me sneeze. Thanks, Brother Harry." John thought back to other years, and then he spoke again. "When I was little, my mother and my sister wrapped me in a feather comforter when it was cold. They thought it was the cold that made me sick; and all along it was probably the comforter."

"Elder Grove knew there had to be something else making you sick. I'll send him word that it was feathers."

John was feeling so happy that he had the courage to ask for a favor. "Would you ask him if I could work in the wood shop?"

A few days later Brother Harry brought the answer. "Elder Grove thinks that sawdust may make you wheeze," he said.

John's heart sank to his toes. He wanted so much to learn to make beautiful Shaker furniture and boxes. He straightened his shoulders and looked straight into Brother Harry's eyes. "Remember how I sanded those handles for boxes? I didn't wheeze then."

"You were sitting on a bench outside of the shop. Inside, the sawdust would be much thicker, just as the feathers were thicker in the chicken house." He handed John a handkerchief and smiled. "Elder Grove knows how much you want

to work with wood. You are to soak this handkerchief in water and tie it around your nose and mouth before you enter the woodworking shop tomorrow after breakfast."

"Tomorrow after breakfast?" John wanted to do a Shaker dance. He lifted his cupped hands in the "gathering" motion. He was gathering blessings from Brother Harry and Elder Grove.

"Keep the handkerchief damp. It will catch some of the sawdust. Wear it all the time you are in the shop for two days. Then, if you are not coughing, you can work for an hour without it. Each day that you don't cough, you will increase the time without it. Maybe you won't need it at all. Maybe you'll only need it when you are doing certain jobs. We'll see."

At the end of the last day of the school term, Sister Lucy Jane asked Hope to remain in the schoolhouse while the others went back to the dwelling. The two of them cleaned the slate board and stacked all of the books neatly on the shelves. Then the teacher sat down at her desk and nodded toward a desk on the front row. Although it was much too small, Hope squeezed into it.

"Your behavior during the last six weeks has pleased the ministry," Sister Lucy Jane said. "We have told the eldresses that you have been a cheerful and willing companion to Sister Hannah and that you are a diligent worker. I have told them that you are bright and an excellent student. That, I remind you, is nothing to be proud of. Intelligence is a gift from God, which we are expected to use wisely—and humbly. I worry that you question too much. Faith comes more easily to those who think less. You will be relieved of your daily duty to Sister Hannah."

"I like Sister Hannah. I—" Hope had forgotten that sitting with the old sister was a punishment.

"I told them you would miss your visits with her, and they gave you permission to stop by Sister Hannah's room, for no more than fifteen minutes a day."

"I can't read much in fifteen minutes," Hope said. "Sister Hannah likes to be read to."

Sister Lucy Jane sighed. "When are you going to learn not to question our every decision? Eldress Dana has given you a special privilege, designed to please you. Accept it with grace. May I tell her that you are pleased and send her your thanks?"

Hope nodded. "Yes, Sister Lucy Jane," she said meekly.

"You will be working in the kitchen during most of the rest of the summer. So will I." Sister Lucy Jane rose and she and Hope walked across the road to the dwelling house together.

* * *

The haying was finished in early August. The next day was special. All the boys, including John, were packed into a wagon for a "surprise" outing. Brother Harry wouldn't tell them where they were going, but they knew they were going some distance because baskets of food were packed in among them. The horses pulled the wagon up hills and down, on straight roads and curved, until they arrived at a sparkling lake. They spent the whole day hiking around the lake, swimming and fishing. They built a fire and cooked their fish for supper, and then they headed home.

"This was one of the best days of my whole life," John murmured sleepily to Calvin as they bumped along toward home.

7

Hope spent the hot summer months working in the kitchen. The kitchen was on the bottom level of the dwelling and partly underground. In spite of the fires needed for cooking and baking, the kitchen was not as hot as Hope would have expected. There were windows and breezes. The stones in the foundation stayed cool until the very end of the summer.

Hope laid out fruits to dry and helped make peach and plum jam. She learned to roll pie crust so that it would just fit the pan.

Some days she and many girls and a few sisters were sent into the fields with tow sheets. They picked one specific herb until the sheets were filled. They picked more sage than any other herb; it was a "money crop" to be sold to people in the outside world. Some of the herbs were used to flavor foods; others were used as medicines.

During August and September, John sometimes worked outside, digging potatoes, pulling up bean plants, and picking early apples. More often, he was sent to the wood shop.

After a short time he no longer wore the damp handkerchief over his nose. Sawdust did not cause him to wheeze, or even to sneeze. He smoothed wood and fetched tools for the brothers, and watched them work.

In September he started work on a project of his own, a milking stool. Although he needed help with the lathe, he did most of the work himself. The stool had to be as steady and as smooth and as carefully finished as the benches in the meeting house. That's the way the Shakers were. Nothing was fancy and nothing was second rate.

When his stool was finished, he took it to the round barn. It was just like the other milking stools so that when the newness wore off, John could not tell which stool he had made. Still it gave him pleasure to know that he had made something the brothers could use.

As summer turned to fall, bursts of warm weather alternated with bursts of cold. Each night fell earlier, and each morning dawned later.

Hope envied the geese as they flew overhead in their giant V formation, honking farewells to the people on the ground. Except for the night in Fay's barn, she had not been off Shaker land since they had arrived in February. She felt as if she were on a leash. Sometimes she imagined breaking free, spreading her arms and running on and on down the road until she was miles from this place.

Squirrels scurried about, scolding as they stored their nuts. The sisters were busy preserving the last vegetables from the garden. The hour for rising was pushed forward so that the morning bell wasn't rung until five thirty. Winter clothes were brought down from the attics and aired and pressed. Summer clothes were washed and those that could be used another season were stored. Faded and worn clothing was sent to the sewing room to be made into something else. The brothers prepared the fields for the coming winter. They split and stacked wood to feed the stoves.

The Berkshire Hills that surrounded the Shaker Village were the same hills Hope had cherished when she lived with Ma and Pa. In the middle of October they blazed with the colors of fire, scarlet and gold, interrupted here and there by the green of a fir or a pine.

One morning, when the colors were most vivid, Sister Anna told the girls to put on their Sabbath dresses and bring their cloaks downstairs. That's all she would say. After breakfast they went out into the yard. Two wagons waited, each with a pair of brothers on the high seat behind a pair of horses. Sister Lucy Jane led half of the girls and two sisters to one wagon; Sister Anna took the other half of the girls and another sister to the second wagon. No one spoke a word. Hope took her place on the back end of a bench beside Catherine. The first wagon began to move. The second one followed, jolting across the yard to the road and then west away from the village.

At last Hope was leaving Hancock Shaker Village! The horses trotted along until they came to the first long hill. As they strained to pull the heavy load of women and girls up the hill, they slowed until the wagon was barely moving. It would be nothing for me to jump over the back of this wagon and run off into the woods, Hope thought. And after that? She had no money, and soon it would be winter. She wondered if anyone would look for her if she were alone as they had looked for her when she was with John.

"God must love us very much to give us

such beauty," Catherine whispered to Hope, her eyes shining.

"Maybe. Or maybe He's apologizing in advance for the cold miserable weather He has in store for us." Hope smiled at Catherine's idea, and at her own. "Is this the first time you have left Hancock?"

"Nay. I've been to New Lebanon many times. That's where we're going now. After dinner we'll visit with the girls there. I'll see Amy and Bertha. They're like me, practically born Shakers."

It had never occurred to Hope that Catherine would have friends outside of Hancock. "Have you been to any of the other communities?"

"I've been to Enfield in Connecticut twice with the eldresses. The second time we stayed three nights. Eldress Dana said that one day I may be able to go on a long trip to New Hampshire and Maine. Have you ever been outside of Massachusetts?"

Hope shook her head. "But one day I am going all the way across the country to California."

They stopped talking and raised their faces to the warm sun.

"You've been outside of Massachusetts now," Catherine whispered as they turned off the broad road to a narrower one. "New

Lebanon is in New York State and we are almost there."

The village at New Lebanon was larger than the one at Hancock. The buildings were similar, but bigger, and there were more of them. The Church family at New Lebanon was the center for the thousands of Shakers who lived in communities from Maine to Kentucky and Connecticut to Ohio.

The day went as Catherine had said it would. The dinner was good, but Hope thought that the bread was not as fine as Hancock bread. She did not like any of the girls as much as she had liked Jemima—or Catherine.

On the way home, she prodded and poked at a new idea. She needed to know what had happened to her father. If she and John were to be placed with the Shakers in Ohio or Kentucky they would be part way to California. And they would be among people to whom Hope had made no promises. She sometimes wished that she had not promised the Hancock eldresses that she would stay.

"Do you know anyone who's ever been transferred from one village to another?" she asked Catherine.

"They sent Justina and Elizabeth to another village after the sheriff brought them back to wait for the court hearing."

"I wonder what the judge decided." Hope hadn't thought of the Irving sisters for a long time.

"The judge took them away from us. He said they belonged to their nasty father. Poor Justina and Elizabeth. They must be so very sad."

"Do you know others who have been sent from one village to another?"

"A sick child was moved to New Lebanon where she could be nursed better. Adults are moved, sometimes, to villages that need their special talents."

"What if you asked to be moved?"

"Why would anyone want to do that?" Catherine looked puzzled.

Hope shrugged. "To see more of the country. You said yourself you'd like to go to Maine."

"For a visit. I wouldn't want to live there."

In the weeks that followed, Hope thought often about the wagon trip, wondering why she had not run when she had the chance. The answer was always the same. It would soon be winter and she had no money and no place to go. Furthermore, she could not leave without John. And she had promised to stay.

One day everyone, except for Sister Hannah and a few others who were very old, went to the orchard to pick apples. Men and women together! It was a party, and they ate their dinner out under the trees. John was there. After dinner he climbed a tree and threw apples down to Hope. One of the brothers walked by and looked at them, but he didn't call John away. That was a surprise.

The biggest surprise was John. His cheeks were round and rosy like the apples they were picking. His eyes were bright.

"I'm a healthy lad," he said with a grin. "Just as long as I stay away from hay and feathers."

"Feathers? You mean feathers in a chicken house or feathers in a comforter?"

"Both. And feathers in a pillow. Brother Harry found a new pillow for me. It's as soft as a block of wood, but I don't have to blow my nose when I wake up." He told Hope about their outing to the lake and about the box he was making. "I wish I could give it to you," he said.

"I wish you could, too. Do you miss Pa?"

John furrowed his brow. "I can't remember what Pa looked like," he said.

"You can't remember Pa?" She was shocked and angry. "Remember how he rode you around on his shoulders and you shouted 'Giddy-up'? Remember how he called you 'My boy'? He always said it so proudly. 'This is my boy, John.' I won't let you forget our pa. We have to go find him, both of us, together!" She shouted at John as an even more disturbing thought crept into her brain. "You haven't forgotten Ma, have you?"

"Nay, Hope. I remember Ma. She was so sick, and she lay in the bed and her skin looked yellow."

"That's how you think of her? You must remember when she and Pa danced together. Not silly Shaker dancing but real dancing. And we danced, too. You and me."

"I don't remember, Hope." He climbed down from the tree and looked into her face. "I'm sorry, Hope." He climbed another tree and began to throw apples down to an old brother.

She dropped down on the ground and buried her head in her knees. These crazy Shakers had made John forget his real family!

The next week, Hope was sent to work in the herb house for the first time. Bunches of herbs hung from racks in the ceiling and were crammed into huge baskets on the floor and tables. Many of them were colorful, and the mixture of odors made the herb house as fragrant as the kitchen.

The work itself was boring; she spent days stripping dried leaves from stiff stems. But the sisters working with the herbs chattered.

Sister Amelia, who was in charge, had interesting things to say about the herbs.

Hope had admired lobelia's pretty blue flowers, and she had enjoyed the day they had picked the lobelia. Sister Amelia said that the leaves and seeds could be used to treat many ailments. At New Lebanon they grew fields of lobelia, which they dried and packed into bars that were shipped all over the world. At Hancock the sisters only prepared enough for their own needs.

"We have a new boy with asthma," Sister Amelia said, "so we barely had enough lobelia to get us through the year. We'll prepare more this year."

"The boy is my brother," Hope whispered. "I didn't know lobelia would be good for him."

"It takes someone who knows to give just the right dose of lobelia when it goes inside the body. When it goes on the outside, I always say the more the better. There's nothing like a good strong lobelia paste for sprains or bites or poison ivy. Remember this, young Hope, if you should feel poison ivy bumps rising on your skin, get lobelia on it, in whatever form, just as fast as possible."

The sisters around the table all nodded in agreement.

Every day, Sister Amelia explained the uses of the herb they were preparing.

Sometimes she asked Hope questions to see if she remembered what she had been told on previous days.

"You have an inquiring mind," she said to Hope. "And you remember what you have been told. We appreciate that."

The sisters around the table all nodded in agreement.

Several of the sisters working in the herb house told stories about people who had been cured with this or that herb or treatment. They recalled sisters long dead and sympathized with the afflictions of other members of the village, particularly Elder Grove, who had a skin problem.

"We've tried everything we can think of to relieve his itching," Sister Amelia said. "Sometimes we find a lotion that works for a while, but just as we begin to hope we've found a cure, the rash comes back. Lobelia was effective for a time."

The sisters also shared information that had nothing to do with health and herbs. Hope wondered how they knew so much about the brothers. Then she remembered that the sisters sometimes went to union meetings. Hope had once passed an open door and seen six sisters sitting in a row of chairs opposite four brothers. She had wondered what they talked about. Now she knew because the herb house sisters shared what they heard at union meetings with one another.

They reported on the travels of the elders and deacons. They said that the trustees wanted the boys to make more brushes than they had last year because there was such a demand for them in the outside world. They said that their dear child Calvin Fairchild was growing into a fine young man. And then they explained to Hope that he had been left outside their dwelling when he was just a baby.

"No one knows how he got there and no one ever came to claim him, so we gave him a birthday and a name. Calvin is a gift."

"Is Catherine a gift, too? She's been here since she was a baby."

"Oh yes. All of our children are gifts from God, but Catherine and Calvin came to us so young that we can't help feeling that they are marked for something special."

"What about Jemima?" Hope whispered, and then bit her tongue. It wasn't kind of her to ask that question, knowing that the Shakers were forbidden to gossip.

Sister Amelia smiled at Hope. "Poor Jemima. We need women with spirit and energy. Jemima had both. We hoped she would learn to conform to our ways. Now, I fear, she is lost."

"What if she came back?"

"She would be welcomed into the fold. We never turn anyone away. I hope she knows that. I hate to think of her out in the cold world, alone. From what we've heard about Zeke, I can't imagine that he is caring for her. The brethren say that they never had confidence in him."

"What if he came back?"

"If he came back, he would be welcomed."

The sisters all nodded and sighed.

Most mornings before she started work at the herb house, Hope visited Sister Hannah. Sometimes she only had time to wave to her from the doorway. Sometimes she repeated the news she had heard the day before.

Hope continued to work in the herb house except for one day when she was sent to the kitchen to peel apples for the last barrel of sauce for that year. The kitchen sisters were so silent that Hope was especially glad to return to the buzz of the herb house.

"It's the coldest, windiest November I can remember," Sister Amelia announced one morning.

The sisters nodded in agreement, and a sister who was no bigger than most ten-year-olds giggled. "If Sister Amelia and Hope hadn't held my arms, I might have just flown off in a whirlwind. Wouldn't that have surprised

Mother Ann, to find me rapping at the door of heaven before I'd been called?"

They all smiled, and Hope once again marveled at how they talked about Mother Ann as if she were in the next room. Only a few who were very old, like Sister Hannah, had actually seen this woman they all loved so dearly.

8

On the last day of November it snowed three inches—and Sister Hannah was not sitting in her chair when Hope went up to see her. She waited a few minutes; the old lady might be using the commode. Then she went next door to the infirmary and saw Sister Chloe bending over a bed.

With fear clutching at her throat, Hope crept into the room toward the bed. Sister Chloe looked up and beckoned to her to approach the bed where Sister Hannah lay, her wrinkled cheeks sunken and pale. When she saw Hope, she reached out her gnarled hand to Hope but she did not speak. Hope held the hand for a few minutes. It was cold and limp, so she tucked it under the blanket and stood silently beside the bed.

"Please get better," Hope begged.

The corners of Sister Hannah's mouth twitched as if they wanted to smile, and then the old lady began to cough, and Sister Chloe sent Hope away.

Sister Lucy Jane gave Hope permission to visit Sister Hannah a second time during the day, but the old lady never opened her eyes while Hope was there.

Two days later, when Hope went to the infirmary, Sister Hannah was raised up on pillows and looking brighter. The two other beds in the room were also occupied by sisters who had deep chest coughs. Sister Chloe was not with them.

"Gone to the sick brothers," one of the sisters said between coughs.

By the end of the next week, five rooms on the second floor of the dwelling had been set aside for the sick: the infirmary and two others for sisters and two across the hall for brothers.

Sister Lydia Hoyt, the large woman with the beautiful voice, left her job in the office to nurse the sick. It was she who had taken Hope's locket on the day Uncle Josiah had brought them to Hancock. Sister Lydia marched and Sister Chloe scampered among their patients, steaming them and giving emetics and plasters and cough medicine.

Hope went every morning to visit Sister Hannah, who began to look healthier than the new patients. Several times Sister Chloe asked Hope to pour herb and honey tea from the pots that were kept on top of the black stoves. "Tell Sister Amelia that we are so busy up here that we had to have your help. She'll excuse you for being late."

A brother was on duty in the sickrooms across the hall. Sister Molly, who was not more than a few years older than Hope, was sent upstairs to help the nurses. Still Hope poured tea for the sick before she went to the herb house.

One morning while she was pouring tea, Hope heard a wracking cough. It was Sister Chloe, coughing and clutching the door. Hope reached her as she sank toward the floor.

In the middle of the room, Sister Molly stood wringing her hands. "Oh dear, oh dear," she whimpered.

"Come help me," Hope said.

Sister Molly did not move.

"Go get Sister Lydia." Hope eased Sister Chloe to a sitting position on the floor and held her tightly as the old sister continued to cough.

"Oh dear me." Sister Molly continued to wring her hands.

"Go get Sister Lydia," Hope repeated. "Now."

At last one of the sick sisters climbed from her bed, wrapped a shawl around her shoulders and went out into the hall. Within minutes Sister Lydia was at the doorway. Together, she and Hope helped Sister Chloe to an empty bed in the next room.

Sister Molly traipsed after them, still wringing her hands. "What if you'd been tending to one of the men? I couldn't go after you. I just didn't know ... Oh dear, oh dear."

"In an emergency we do what must be done. Now go get Sister Chloe's nightgown and bring it to us."

"Oh dear, oh dear." Sister Molly was crying, but she left the room and returned with the nightgown.

Sister Lydia took the nightgown. While she was putting it over Sister Chloe's head she spoke softly. "Put on your cloak, Sister Molly, and go directly to the herb house. Tell Sister Amelia that I must have Hope's help. Then find Sister Anna and tell her the same thing. Sister Chloe is sick, and I must have adequate help, Hope's help."

Sister Chloe's teeth were chattering and her forehead was burning. Her body was limp. When she was tucked snugly into the bed, Sister Lydia went to steam the sisters in the next room while Hope poured a cup of tea and held it to the old nurse's lips. Still she shivered. Hope added another blanket and a shawl and went on to tend to the needs of the other sisters in the room.

The health of the sisters and brethren continued to decline until nine of the rooms on the second floor housed patients. Hope slept, when there was time to sleep, in the bed that had been Sister Chloe's before she was taken sick. After a few days, some of the sick seemed well enough to return to their regular rooms and to light work. Within a few days, many of them were back, sicker than they had been before.

There were hardly enough healthy sisters to staff the kitchen and the laundry. The few brothers who were not coughing had all they could do to tend to the animals and keep the woodboxes full. Sister Lucy Jane was keeping the girls separate from the sick, and Sister Anna was helping in the kitchen. Sisters who were still coughing but were otherwise feeling better tended to the needs of the feverish.

Some of the barriers between the brethren and the sisters were even lowered during the emergency. At first Sister Lydia would only allow Hope to care for the sisters. "You must not go across the hall," she said over and over. "And you must not get sick yourself," she always added. Hope did not get sick herself, but long before the end of December she was caring for the sick on both sides of the hall.

The first boy to need care was Calvin Fairchild. Hope had heard so much about him from her brother and from the sisters in the herb house that she had expected someone who looked like a cross between George Washington and an angel. Instead Calvin Fairchild looked like an ordinary boy except that his hair was almost white and his eyes were bright blue.

"I'm Hope Douglas, John's sister," she said as she brought him the mixture of herbs they were giving to all of the sick. He started to say something and then he began to cough so that he could not speak. Neither could he swallow the herbs that had been made into giant pills.

She took horehound from her pocket and gave him a piece to suck while she rubbed his back. At last he stopped coughing. "John's well," he whispered.

Please, God, keep him well, Hope prayed silently.

Every morning she looked into all of the sickrooms hoping not to see John.

It was the custom to celebrate Jesus's birthday in December in the same way that they had celebrated Mother Ann's birthday on March 1, with marches and meetings. But by December 24, so many were sick that the elders announced that Jesus's day would be a day like any other except that all were asked to offer special prayers for the sick.

When the first bell sounded at five thirty on Christmas morning, Hope was too tired to open her eyes. She couldn't remember how many times she had been up in the night to tend to the sick. When she could no longer ignore the coughs coming from the sick-rooms, she turned her head. Sister Lydia's body was so large that when she lay down she looked like a mountain on top of her narrow bed. Her bed was empty and the blankets had been thrown back to air. Hope sighed and stretched and forced herself to get up and dressed and then she put a smile on her face.

Some of the sisters seemed better and she was feeling almost cheerful until she came to Sister Hannah's bed. The old lady's skin was whiter than the sheet. Her body was perfect-ly still except for the uneven rise and fall of her chest. Hope smoothed a few strands of white hair away from her wrinkled forehead. It felt clammy.

"Sister Hannah," Hope whispered. "It's me, Hope."

Sister Hannah's lips moved but she did not open her eyes.

Sister Lydia came into the room and stood beside Hope. "It's time to wish our sister a joyful voyage," she said.

Alarmed, Hope turned to stare at Sister Lydia. "No," she protested, wondering at the nurse's cheerful smile.

"Yea," Sister Lydia said firmly and left the room.

"I will lift up mine eyes unto the hills, from whence cometh my help," Hope said, remembering the first afternoon she had spent with Sister Hannah. She choked on the words that followed. Sadness, like a great black cloak, fell upon her. And then the sister in the next bed began to cough.

Hope returned to Sister Hannah's bedside many times during the day. She never opened her eyes. Late in the afternoon, her breathing stopped.

The next day Hope and those who were well, and some who were still coughing, assembled in the meeting room for Sister Hannah's funeral.

Toward evening, when Hope was serving herbal tea, Sister Chloe took Hope's hand. "Be joyful," she said. "You brightened Sister Hannah's last months. She told me, not just once but many times, that every day was sunnier because she knew you would come smile at her. I am an old woman and I will follow her very soon. Many years from now, when your time comes, Sister Hannah and I will be first in line after Mother Ann to welcome you. Isn't that a happy thought?"

Hope could not feel happy, but she felt better. Two days later, Sister Chloe was back tending to the sick in one room. She was so weak that she used Sister Hannah's wheeled chair to move herself from bed to bed. Calvin Fairchild returned to the boys' house.

"Don't you get sick yourself," Sister Lydia continued to say to Hope at least once every day.

Sister Lydia herself remained healthy and calm. She crooned comforting words, and Hope thought that Sister Lydia's musical voice was as healing as her large hands. If she was tired, she didn't show it. As for Hope, she was even more tired now that Sister Hannah was gone.

Finally there came a day in January when Hope slept all night through. One by one, the sickrooms were emptied and cleaned. Healthy sisters and brethren moved back into them. Everyone moved slowly. Those who had been sick were still weak. Those who had remained well were exhausted.

Sister Chloe insisted that she was well enough to resume all her duties as nurse for the family, but the eldresses decided that it was time to begin to train a younger sister.

"I just wish you were older," Sister Lydia said to Hope. "You will be one of the finest nurses we've ever had. You might go to medical school to learn to be a doctor."

Hope laughed. "You're making fun, Sister Lydia. Girls can't become doctors."

"Maybe yea, maybe nay. One of the trustees said that a woman was graduated from the Geneva Medical School the year before last."

Hope was stunned into silence. She had never considered that a woman could be a doctor, that she herself could be a doctor.

"Think about it, Hope. If anyone were to support a woman who wanted to be a doctor, it would be us. Shakers value their women and elevate them to positions of responsibility. I'm not saying that the eldresses would send you to medical school. I am saying that they would consider what others would consider to be impossible. We'd like to have a doctor who was one of us. Why shouldn't that doctor be a woman—you, to be specific?"

Hope was speechless, bewitched by Sister Lydia's beautiful voice speaking beautiful words.

"In the meantime, I will inform the ministry that you have been a blessing to Sister

Chloe and me and to every one of the sick. We are very grateful to you, Hope."

At that moment, Hope felt happier than she had felt since Pa left for California.

John learned about his sister's nursing services from Calvin. "I heard Sister Lydia say that they could not have managed without Hope," Calvin told John when he returned to their room on the second floor of the boys' house.

"Hope's a good nurse. She took good care of Ma, and she took good care of me, too. I used to be sick a lot. She'd rub my back and wrap me in a feather comforter. She didn't know that feathers made me worse."

"She rubbed my back, too," Calvin said. "And gave me medicine to help me stop coughing."

"How did she look?"

Calvin shrugged. "Like a girl. I don't know. How's she supposed to look?"

"Happy, maybe?"

Again Calvin shrugged. "She wasn't crying."

"Did she look cross?"

"I don't think so. She looked busy, rushed. She didn't have time to tell me how she felt."

"She wouldn't have told you anyway, but you'd have known if she was feeling cross or sad. When Hope is cross she stomps across the room and bangs things together. If she'd rubbed your back when she was feeling cross, she'd have

thumped the air right out of your chest." John grinned. "I hope Hope's happy."

"Hope Hope's happy," Calvin repeated, laughing at the sound of the words. The boys said them together, over and over until they were pup-pup-pupping like a steam engine.

John was happy, especially now that the members of his Shaker family were mostly well. For most of December and January, he had only gone to school part time. Mornings before school he had often shoveled snow from the paths between the buildings. Afternoons he had helped haul logs. These were jobs the brethren usually did, but there weren't enough healthy men to do all that had to be done. Many of the boys were sick, too, but John was not one of them.

In February, life at Hancock returned to normal. John went to school and made brushes and attended meetings. He looked forward to working in the wood shop again. He'd make another box like the one he had finished before the school term started. He wished Hope could see his box.

While Hope had been sleeping on the second floor, changes had been made in the girls' rooms on the third. Two girls had been moved from one of the other rooms to the beds that had once been Jemima's and little Emma's. All of the girls welcomed Hope's return.

"I have prayed that you would be granted

the gift of healing." Eunice smiled smugly and folded her hands.

"I prayed, too," Rachel said. Her smile was as sticky as Eunice's, and she, too, folded her hands.

Poor Rachel, will you never have a thought of your own? Hope asked silently.

"We heard you were a wonderful nurse," Catherine said. "Was it hard, taking care of sick people all day long?"

"Yes. For a long time we never got to sleep through the night. But every time someone got better and could go back to her own room, we felt good. We couldn't cure Sister Hannah. It was like with my mother. No matter how hard I tried, Ma just kept getting sicker. So did Sister Hannah."

"But the other sisters got well." Catherine's smile was real, mostly in her eyes.

"The brothers, too."

"How do you know?" Eunice asked.

"I helped nurse some of them."

Eunice raised her eyes to heaven. "How could you? It's against the rules. I suppose you'll tell me that you touched men." She shivered and made a sour face.

"As a matter of fact, I rubbed the backs of some of them. That was hard because the boys have moss growing on their backs and the men have slime, like frogs."

Eunice and Rachel both stared at Hope, their mouths hanging open. Eunice clutched at her throat. For once she was speechless.

And then Catherine and the two new girls burst into laughter.

"I knew she was lying to us." Eunice sniffed. "Come, Rachel, we will pray for these wicked girls."

Hope had been so busy in January that she had not known one day from the next; she had missed the first anniversary of her mother's death and the anniversary of the day Uncle Josiah had brought them to the Shakers.

On Mother Ann's birthday, however, Hope had time to think back. On that date a year earlier she had expected her stay with the Shakers to be short. She had believed that her father would appear any day to take her and John away to California. That dream had shriveled to nothing, leaving a hole in her heart.

A year ago she had been unhappy and angry; now she was neither sad nor mad—nor was she glad. When she thought about her parents, she grieved for her mother, whom she knew to be dead, and her father, whom she now supposed to be dead. She no longer thought of them every day.

Her pleasures were few and brief, but so

were her sorrows. Sometimes she thought about the woman Sister Lydia said had become a doctor. It would be wonderful to be able to heal sick people. In another half year she would be fourteen and ready to leave the children's order. Perhaps the sisters would allow her to work in the herb house and with the nurses. She seldom thought far into the future.

9

The ugly winter seemed to go on and on. When the boys' school closed on March 16 to free the students for farm work, the fields were still frozen. Almost a foot of snow fell during the last week of March and another four inches fell on April 1. On April 13, when the girls' school started, there was yet another huge snowfall. It had been so cold for so long that many of the sisters looked pale and shriveled. Some still coughed.

God's apology arrived during the first week in May. The sun melted the last trace of snow, and green buds began to swell on the trees and shrubs. At last the peas could be planted and the asparagus poked up through the earth.

On Thursday afternoon Sister Anna came to the schoolhouse and said that Hope was wanted in the ministry. Why? If Sister Anna knew, she did not say. Hope had believed that the sisters were pleased with her; the eldresses could not wish to scold her. Could they?

They smiled at her when she stood in front of them, and then Eldress Dana handed her a piece of paper. "It's a letter from your father," she said. "It seems he has had great difficulty finding you. He sent this letter to the minister of the church your family attended. The minister asked your uncle where you were. Your uncle was reluctant to tell him …"

"Was it a secret?"

"We didn't think so. You should know by now that we are not deceitful. We don't know what your uncle was thinking." The eldress frowned for a moment and then smiled. "Sit over there and read your letter."

The eldresses turned to talk together while Hope sank into a chair and unfolded the paper with trembling hands.

> My dear children,
>
> I take pen in hand to ask once again, Where are you? Why didn't you or someone let me know when your mother was ill? I should have been with her. And now it is too late. You

two are my consolation.

Perhaps you did write and think me a scoundrel because you have not heard from me. Since early spring of last year, I have written you three times, always in care of your uncle Josiah. Perhaps my letters—and the money I enclosed—or your responses have been lost. The mail coach here in the West is not always reliable.

My partner, Charles Clark, will carry this letter to Ohio and mail it to the Reverend Whitcome, who will surely know where you are. I pray that this letter will reach you.

I cannot come myself because one of us must stay to protect our farm. Mr. Clark and I, two lonely family men, met on the trail west of St. Joseph. We panned for gold for a while with moderate success. Contrary to what you may have heard, the streets are not paved with gold. When the stream we were working was exhausted, everyone was anxious to get on to the next big strike. A man who owned most of the old shanty town and forty acres of land sold it to us for the gold we had panned. Right away, we bought a few chickens and planted vegetables—

fresh food being in great demand. The land is good and the seasons are long. No snow! We have now expanded considerably. I have combined the best of several shanties into a snug little house. Oh, I hope you will get this letter!

I am enclosing money so that you can buy train tickets to Cleveland. Mr. Clark or a member of his family will meet you there. He plans to return to California with many wagons filled with his family and their belongings as well as cattle and equipment that we need and items that we hope to sell at a profit. They will be ready to leave Ohio in May so you should be here by September. Be prepared for a long, hard trip. Write Mr. Clark at the address below and tell him when to meet you. He is a man to be trusted.

Until I hold you in my aching arms, I remain your loving father.

When she had finished the letter, Hope jumped to her feet. "May! Mr. Clark might go without us. And where's the money my father sent?"

"Calm yourself," Eldress Dana said. "Mr. Clark wrote Mr. Whitcome that he hopes to leave Ohio during the last week in May. As for the money, we have put it in the office safe for the time being."

"You've got to let me see John and show him Pa's letter. Pa is alive and I have been so worried and now we are going to California and ..." Suddenly tears sprang into Hope's eyes. "I have been so afraid that Pa was dead. We'd be orphans then, John and me." She straightened her shoulders. "So I've got to see John right away."

"John has read the letter. But you see, Hope, John does not want to go to California. He doesn't remember his father. He wants to stay here—"

"You've made John think that he wants to stay here. You don't have children of your own. You want him to be one of your gifts like Calvin Fairchild and Catherine. But John is my brother and Pa's son, and we are going to California. Right away. Today. Tomorrow."

Eldress Dana rose to her feet. "Your behavior is objectionable, Hope Douglas. I will ask Sister Anna to take you to some isolated place in the sunshine where you will hem towels until we gather for supper. During that time, I will expect you to make every effort to think clearly. Think what is best for your brother. Ask yourself if he is strong enough for a treacherous journey. Consider his character and his talents."

"I can't go unless he goes with me. Pa has built a house for us. We're family. What would he think if I told him I'd left my brother behind? You don't care about me; you only want John. Have you locked him up?"

"I will arrange for you to meet with your brother after supper." Sister Dana's eyes flashed with anger. "You are excused. Be sure she hems those towels carefully, Sister Anna."

Hope turned and stomped toward the door.

"One moment, Hope." Eldress Dana's voice was no longer angry. Instead it was sad. "Have you been so miserable with us, Hope? If you think we have valued your brother over you, you are mistaken. You are strong and compassionate and bright. I pray daily that you will adopt our faith." Suddenly the eldress smiled. "You are also obstinate and willful but so, too, was our dear Mother Ann. Go now and think of us. Ask yourself if ours is not a life that would bring you peace—and joy."

Hope swallowed and nodded. Then she ran down the stairs ahead of Sister Anna. She hurried across the road and leaned against a chestnut tree, burying her head in her arms while she kicked the trunk until her toes hurt. Why did Eldress Dana have to be so loving? She was trying to confuse Hope, making her think she could stay here and be happy. Hope knew where she belonged. She belonged with her real family, her brother and her father, not this Shaker family. She kicked the trunk again.

After some minutes, Sister Anna put her hand on Hope's shoulder and turned her away from the tree toward a bench. She handed her a towel and a threaded needle. Hope sat and jabbed the needle into the cloth.

"I am ashamed of you," Sister Anna hissed. "You have been taken into our family and loved. Can't you be grateful?" Hope said nothing. "Your brother has also been loved. His body has grown strong here. I have heard that he has expressed delight in our work and our ways. He's a gentle little boy. You, Hope, have been harsh in your criticism of us. Have you ever been treated with anything but kindness? How dare you accuse the elders of cruelty to John?"

Hope did not answer, and she and Sister Anna sewed in silence. Hope had waited a year for this day when she would hear from Pa. It was good to think of him in California, raising vegetables and chickens where the soil was rich and it never snowed. But his letter also told her that he was lonely. He was sad because he had not known that Ma was sick and his arms ached for his children. They had to go to him, no matter how hard the journey! John would understand that.

Before they came here, she could convince John to do anything she wanted him to do. Once she had even made him go alone to a neighbor to beg for potatoes for Ma. He was only eight years old, and he had cried, saying it was too cold and too far, but he had gone. She thought about how Sister Lucy Jane treated the poor little girls from the neighboring farm. She hugged them and praised them and fed them. By contrast, Hope had been harsh with John. When she saw him after supper, she would promise to treat him kindly, all the way to California.

John had spent most of the day planting beets and thinking about the letter from his father. He had read it three times, trying to remember the man who had written it and thinking of chickens and vegetables and a long, hard trip by wagon all the way across the country. At last he had looked up at Elder Grove, who was smiling at him.

"I don't want to go," John had said.

"You don't have to." Those few words had made John's heart sing. "But if you stay now, you'll have to stay until you are twenty-one. Then you can decide for the rest of your life."

"I'll stay forever and ever," John had said.

Elder Grove had laughed aloud and ruffled John's hair. "We'll see."

John hadn't even thought about Hope until

this morning. Maybe she'd want to stay with the Shakers, too. But then he'd have to worry about Pa. Hope liked to go places. John hoped that she would go to Pa.

He thought about the woodworking shop, the benches and the tools and the brothers who worked there. The stool he made was used every day by the men and boys who milked the cows. He'd made one box and started another. One day he might be allowed to make a clock. Wouldn't that be something? Would Hope understand how much he wanted to make a clock and a table and a chest of drawers?

After supper Brother Benjamin took him to a union meeting in one of the rooms on the first floor of the brick dwelling. John had never been to a union meeting, but he knew that it was the one time the brothers and the sisters talked together. He and Brother Benjamin and two other brothers stood in front of a row of chairs. Hope and three sisters came in and stood in front of four chairs about four feet away from the brothers. They all sat down at once.

"We are here so that Hope Douglas can talk with her brother John Douglas," one of the sisters said.

"I can't talk to him in front of all these people." Hope sounded cross and unhappy, which made John uneasy.

"You'll have to, Hope. Just say whatever it is you want to say to John. Ask him any questions." The sister smiled first at Hope and then at John.

For a moment Hope said nothing, and then she turned to look directly in his face. "Pa needs us, Johnny. You read his letter. He's lonely, and now that Ma is dead we're all he's got. We're a family, Pa and you and me, and we belong together. That's what Ma wanted for us. You have to do what Ma wanted. So tell everyone here that we're going. We need train tickets, and we'll be on our way. Tomorrow."

"I don't want to go." John's voice quivered but he spoke loudly.

"You have to go." Suddenly Hope smiled. "Come on, Johnny. You know you have to obey Pa. I know I didn't always treat you right, considering you were so little. I'm 'specially sorry about making you go to the Blackwoods' that time to ask for potatoes. You cried and it was already getting dark and I...I didn't know what else to do. But I'll be kind in the future. I promise. Come with me and I'll be so nice you won't even know me. Please, John. I want to go to California, and I can't go without you."

For a minute, John was afraid he was going to cry. That would not do. He had to show her that he was almost a man now and old enough to decide for himself. "Why can't you go without me, Hope?"

"I promised Ma I'd take care of you. How can

I do that if you are on one side of the country and I am thousands of miles away in California?"

"Brother Harry and Brother Benjamin take care of me. Today I planted beets, but I sometimes spend almost all day in the woodworking shop. There are the most wonderful tools and benches and I made a box and—"

"Surely they have wood in California." Hope was sounding cross again. She just didn't understand how he felt.

"I want to stay here until I am twenty-one years old, and then I expect I'll stay on for the rest of my life. I like it here. Every day when I get up, I know that I will have enough to eat and a place to sleep and I can hope that maybe I'll be sent to the woodworking shop—or to the print shop. I like the print shop, too."

Hope scowled but she said nothing, and John tried again to make her understand. "I can't remember Pa. This is my family now. I sometimes think of Elder Grove as my grandfather. Calvin is my brother. Brother Benjamin puts peppermints on my tongue when I recite well in school. Don't you think that's funny, Hope?"

Hope did not smile. "If you don't go, John, then I can't go."

"Why, Hope?"

"Because I promised Ma and besides, girls can't travel alone."

Sister Lydia spoke for the first time. "We want you to stay with us, Hope. We all recognize that you would be of great value to our community. Your devotion to the sick this winter was remarkable. Eldress Dana has said that if you stay you will be moved to the nurses' shop when you turn fourteen. There is a possibility that you could be sent to medical school."

Hope didn't allow herself to think about becoming a doctor. "We must go to Pa," she insisted.

"You may go, if you like," Sister Lydia said sadly.

"But we will not allow you to take John unless John says that he wants to go," Brother Benjamin added.

"You will have to decide tomorrow." Sister Lucy Jane smiled at Hope. "The eldresses from the central ministry have been planning a trip to the villages in Ohio. You may go with them and we would ask Mr. Clark to meet you at North Union near Cleveland."

"But John …"

"Why don't you think about him?" Brother Benjamin looked like a doll with painted black hair and a rigid back. "I gather that there have been many changes in John's young life. I think that is why he took so quickly to our routine. He told you himself that he likes to know what the morrow will bring."

"That's dull." Hope continued to feel balky.

"Some like adventure; others like routine," Sister Lucy Jane said. "I think we have discussed the matter enough. Before school starts tomorrow morning, I will ask for your decision, Hope."

"And if you have changed your mind, John, I will expect you to tell me," Brother Benjamin said, and then he turned to Hope. "Elder Grove asked me to tell you, Hope, that he will write to your father. He will tell him about our community and explain John's decision. You and your father may write to John—and visit should you come this way again. He will be allowed to write to you twice each year."

"What about Uncle Josiah?" Hope asked suddenly. "Does he know about this?"

"He is not to be consulted. We believe that he may have received previous letters—perhaps money—from your father, which he failed to pass on to us and to you. Your father will deal with him as he chooses."

Could that be? Could Uncle Josiah have taken Pa's money for himself and his own children?

Hope lay awake most of the night. When morning came she told Sister Lucy Jane that she would go to California, alone if John still insisted on staying in Hancock.

Hope did not tell the other girls about her departure until Sunday afternoon. Monday morning she put on a clean cotton dress and her work shoes and said good-bye to them.

"Poor Hope," Eunice simpered. "You were not graced with the piety demanded by our dear Mother Ann, but I will pray for you."

"I'll pray, too," Rachel said.

Hope smiled at Rachel as she thought how lucky the child was to be with the Shakers. In the outside world someone might tell her to rob a bank or set fire to a barn or jump off a roof. Here no one would ever suggest that she do anything dangerous or wicked. She would always be protected.

"Good-bye, Hope. I trust you will be safe on that long trip," Catherine whispered. "And remember, you will always be welcome to come back to us."

Hope opened her arms and hugged Catherine, thinking that she was indeed a gift. She wondered if one day Catherine would be an eldress.

After breakfast, Sister Anna took Hope to Sister Lydia's office. It was here that Hope had entered the Shaker community and here that she would leave. Clothing hung from the pegs in the room. Sister Lydia took down a new brown cotton dress and showed it to Hope.

"We thought it would be good for travel," she said. "This will be your good dress," she said as she removed a blue dress from a peg and folded it carefully. On top of it she placed underwear, petticoats, and two nightgowns. She showed Hope a pair of sturdy boots—a size larger than her last shoes—and shawls and an old cloak, which she would probably not need except in the mountains. Sister Lydia put everything into a small trunk.

And then she opened a Shaker box on her desk. Inside were packets of seeds and herbs. "Who knows when you may be asked to help someone who is sick? We hope these herbs will be of use to you. Plant the seeds and write us to let us know which ones will thrive in that strange new land where it never snows. Your brother made the box. He wanted you to have it."

Hope was so choked that she could not speak. "Why?" She finally breathed, pointing to the box and the trunk.

"You have been one of ours, dear Hope. We do not want you to go into the world ill-equipped." Sister Lydia placed the box in the trunk and closed it with leather straps and buckles.

Then she removed a folded paper from a drawer and opened it. "As promised," she said as she handed Hope's locket to Sister Anna, who placed it around Hope's neck and fastened it. She tied three gold coins into a cloth. "We will give part of your father's money to the New Lebanon ministry to pay for your expenses on the way to Ohio. These coins are also from your father. I would suggest that you give them to Mr. Clark for safekeeping until you need them. In the meantime, pin them into your petticoat."

Impulsively, Hope kissed Sister Lydia. "Thank you," she said, wishing that she could say more.

Sister Anna picked up the trunk and carried it to the door. "Come," she said. "The wagon is waiting."

An old brother was driving the wagon; two sisters sat on a seat behind him. Sister Lucy Jane stood beside the horse.

I could change my mind, Hope said to herself as she walked across the yard. Perhaps nowhere else in the world will I find such kind people. But even as she thought about these people, she was picturing the wagon train crossing the high mountains to California and Pa.

"Thank you," she said to Sister Anna and to Sister Lucy Jane. She kissed them, too.

Sister Lucy Jane's cheek was damp. So was Hope's.

She walked around the wagon, and there stood John. He smiled up at the man standing beside him. "Brother Harry said we could say good-bye to each other." He turned to Hope. "Wasn't that nice of him? Don't tell Pa that I couldn't remember him, Hope. That might hurt his feelings. You're supposed to take these letters to him. They are copies of letters Elder Grove and I mailed. We hope he'll get them before you get there. But if he doesn't, you'll give him the copies. The letters explain why I am staying. Do you like my box, Hope? Will you take it all the way to California?"

"It's beautiful, and I will keep it for..." She choked and could say no more so she reached out her arms and hugged her brother close. There was so much more of him to hug than there had been a year ago. She'd tell Pa that. "Good-bye, John," she whispered. "Don't forget me and Ma."

He wiggled out of her arms. "Nay. I won't forget." He smiled broadly. "Good-bye, Hope." He turned and walked away with Brother Harry.

She stared after him and climbed into the back of the wagon. The driver clucked at the horse, who trotted out to the road and headed west.

❦ Fact and Fiction ❦

You may be wondering if the story you have just read is true. The answer is both yes and no. Hope, John, members of their family, and most of the Shaker characters were born in my imagination. They live only in the pages of this book. However, when I have given the last name of a Shaker, it is the name of someone who really lived at Hancock Shaker Village in 1851. Some of the events are true.

For example, Calvin Fairchild was found abandoned under a tree near the brick dwelling in 1843 when he was about two years old. Years later, a visitor described him as a fair and handsome youth with blue eyes that were both gentle and merry. The Shakers expected him to become one of their leaders but he died of consumption at the age of twenty-six.

The Irving sisters were taken from the Shakers by their father and the sheriff. Ellen Jenkins died January 31, 1851 and her six-year-old sister, Emma, was taken away by Hiram Jenkins on March 26. Did Emma suck her thumb? Perhaps.

There are no pictures of Shakers living at Hancock at that time, but the names and ages of many of them have been recorded. We can tell from Elder Grove Wright's letters that he was jolly, intelligent, and a dedicated Shaker. He was also a fine woodworker and he brought several orphans to the village. I am sure that he would have welcomed a child like John. Cassandana Brewster, often called Eldress Dana, and Elder Thomas Damon were also members of the ministry.

Sister Lydia Hoyt was an office sister as well as a nurse. I pictured her as a large woman with a beautiful speaking voice, but it is just as likely that she was tiny with a squeaky voice. Lucy Jane Osborne was a teacher in 1851; a few years later she became an eldress. Chloe Slosson was a nurse who died in 1853 at the age of 79.

Journals and letters written by members of the Hancock community and of the near-by Shaker village at Mount Lebanon (called

New Lebanon until 1861) recorded the details of daily life. They tell the exact days school sessions started and ended, what crops were planted and when, how many sisters worked in the kitchen, and how many barrels of applesauce they prepared. They also tell about a disease, probably influenza, that swept through both villages in the winter of 1851-52.

Hope and John didn't know much about the Shakers when they were taken to live at Hancock. What they learn in this novel is true to my understanding of the spirit of Shakerism at that time.

The founder of the Shaker faith was Ann Lee, an uneducated English woman born in 1736. She married a blacksmith and gave birth to four children. When all of her babies died, she decided that God was punishing her. She began to have dreams and visions. She announced that she was God's daughter, just as Jesus was His son. She said that people who wanted to be free from sin had to give up everything, even their families. Men and women could not be married or have close contact with those of the opposite sex.

Ann Lee's followers were called Shakers because they worshiped God with such fervor that their bodies shook as they whirled and stomped their feet. In England they were so noisy and their ideas were thought to be so strange that they were sometimes jailed for disturbing the peace.

While she was in prison, Ann Lee had a vision in which she saw crowds of people waiting for her in America. She and eight of her followers arrived in New York City in 1774 and later acquired land near Albany, New York. They traveled throughout New York and New England, preaching to all who would listen.

Many Americans feared the early Shakers. Since they came from England during the Revolutionary War, they were accused of spying. Their teachings caused the breakup of families. Their worship was rowdy; somber Americans believed that the only way to worship God was to sit or kneel quietly with heads bowed. Mother Ann and her followers were driven from villages, stoned and imprisoned. Still they attracted more and more followers, including clergymen and other respected citizens.

Soon after Mother Ann Lee's death in 1784, groups of her followers began to live together in villages. All new members brought whatever they owned to be shared by the whole community. Many had nothing; others brought thriving farms. Early Shakers report that they were often cold and hungry, but it was not long before the villages began to prosper. Their goal was to provide everything they needed for themselves. Glass and china were among the few things they bought from the outside world.

During the first half of the 1800s, the Society grew until there were more than 4,000 Shakers living in eighteen villages from Maine to Kentucky and as far west as Ohio. During the next hundred years, the numbers gradually decreased; one by one the villages were closed. Today there are only a few people still living together in the Shaker village of Sabbathday Lake, Maine. There have been other communal living groups in the United States, but none has had so many members or lasted so long.

In all of the villages, men and boys were kept completely separate from women and girls. They worked in separate shops. The buildings they shared had separate doors for men and women. Dining rooms and meeting rooms were divided. Although men and women were kept apart from one another, they had equal rights and responsibilities. The leaders of each village were two elders and two eldresses.

Shakers did not give birth to children, but there were children in every village. Some came when their families joined the Shakers. Others were orphans who had nowhere else to go. Many were signed over to the Shakers by their parents so that they would be cared for and taught a trade.

Years ago I met three old people whose fathers had worked for the Shakers at Mount Lebanon. One was a gruff retired state trooper. His parents had been raised by the Shakers, but they had run away so they could marry. When the trooper was four years old, his father had been asked to come back to manage the herb business. The other two were sisters whose father had managed the farm. One of them told me that the happiest days of her life had been days she had gone with a Shaker sister to pick herbs. All three said the same thing at different times: "Oh how the Shaker sisters loved me!"

Many Shakers were fine craftsmen. They did not believe in decorations, but their buildings and furniture were elegant as well as sturdy and convenient. Today many of the buildings are still in use. Shaker furniture is displayed by museums, cherished by private collectors, and copied by craftsmen.

Other Shakers were clever inventors who made the first flat brooms, the first wrinkle-resistant fabrics, and many other practical devices.

They were excellent farmers and the first Americans to package top quality seeds for sale outside of the villages. The Shakers also grew, collected, and sold herbs for cooking and for healing.

Hancock Shaker Village was established in 1790 and grew until there were more than 300 Shakers gathered in six families. In 1960, when only a few sisters remained, the village was sold to a nonprofit group interested in preserving the Shaker heritage.

The round barn, the brick dwelling, and many of the other buildings that were part of the Church family at Hancock have been preserved or restored. The rooms and shops are furnished, the fields and gardens are planted, and cows and sheep graze in the pastures. The boys' house was destroyed sometime in the past but an old map shows where it was. No one knows for sure where the girls lived in 1851; they *may* have lived on the third floor of the large brick dwelling.

Hancock Shaker Village is located just west of Pittsfield, Massachusetts, near the New York border. It is open to individual visitors and to groups. Shaker crafts are often demonstrated; Shaker food is sometimes served. There are also Shaker museums in New York, Ohio, Kentucky, Maine, and New

Hampshire. Some art museums have collections of Shaker furniture. Books about the Shakers, many with lovely pictures, are available in most libraries and bookstores.